Peter Henderson

Peter Henderson's Spring Catalogue of New, Rare and Beautiful Plants

for 1875 - greenhouses at Jeresy City Heights, N.J. - Post office address at

seed store, no. 35 Cortlandt Street, New York

Peter Henderson

Peter Henderson's Spring Catalogue of New, Rare and Beautiful Plants
*for 1875 - greenhouses at Jeresy City Heights, N.J. - Post office address at seed
store, no. 35 Cortlandt Street, New York*

ISBN/EAN: 9783337390600

Printed in Europe, USA, Canada, Australia, Japan

Cover: Foto ©Andreas Hilbeck / pixelio.de

More available books at **www.hansebooks.com**

ESTABLISHED 1848.

No. 27.   1875.

PETER HENDERSON'S

SPRING CATALOGUE

OF

NEW, RARE AND BEAUTIFUL

PLANTS

FOR

1875.

Greenhouses at Jersey City Heights, N. J.

POST OFFICE ADDRESS AT SEED STORE,

No. 35 Cortlandt Street, New York.

NEW YORK.
PRESS OF MUNROE & METZ. 60 JOHN STREET.
1875.

Please to read this Notice before Ordering.

▸◂

Parties ordering will confer a particular favor by using the "order sheet," as it is a great saving of time to us, as well as insuring the more correct filling of orders; nothing is more annoying when we are crowded with business, than to get orders muddled up through the body of the letter.

The system of packing adopted is now so complete, that although we send out many thousand packages annually to every State and Territory in the Union, it is rare to receive a complaint—not more than one in 300 cases—while we receive hundreds of letters attesting satisfaction at the *light, simple* and *safe* method we practice, and the fine condition in which the plants arrive.

WE BEGIN SHIPPING AS SOON AS OUR CATALOGUE IS ISSUED IN JAN-UARY, AND BY THE PRECAUTIONS TAKEN AGAINST FROST, SELDOM HAVE A CASE INJURED.

Every order is sent *the day after it is received*, unless otherwise ordered; provided the article ordered is in proper condition to send, so that if parties ordering do not receive goods in reasonable time they may be assured the order has not reached us.

All goods are sent by express unless specially ordered otherwise, and we earnestly advise our customers to have their plants always sent by express, as our light system of packing makes the charges comparatively low, and they almost invariably arrive in perfect order when thus sent. The difference between express and freight charges is nothing when the certainty of having them received in good condition, when sent by express, is taken into consideration.

We will send plants by mail as heretofore: but we would here impress upon our patrons the fact, that no plant should ever be sent by mail to any point where an express office reaches, as *larger and finer plants* and *more of them for the same amount*, can be sent by express than by mail; for in all orders from THIS CATALOGUE, sent by express, extra plants are always included that are of more value than cost of expressage.

It will always be to the interest of purchasers to leave the selection of varieties as far as possible to us, when full sets are not taken, as it is very difficult to judge of the merits of varieties by descriptions. When selections are left to us, persons may *always rely on receiving better plants* than if they selected themselves, as perhaps the variety selected we may have no good plants of.

NO CHARGES FOR BOXES, BASKETS, OR PACKING.

Orders from unknown correspondents, unless accompanied by a remittance or satisfactory reference, will be sent by Express, C. O. D. From this rule we make no deviation.

Persons wishing to examine Stock should call at our Seed Store, 35 Cortlandt Street, New York, where a card with directions will be given to reach the greenhouses on Jersey City Heights. Time from Seed Store, 30 minutes by steam cars or 40 minutes by horse cars. I may here say that parties wishing to see me personally, will find me at the greenhouses until 12 o'clock M, and at my office, 35 Cortlandt Street, New York, from 1.30 P. M. to 3.30 P. M.

To those who are strangers to us, into whose hands this Catalogue may come, we beg to say that we are also largely engaged in the SEED BUSINESS; our extensive greenhouses and grounds give us peculiar advantages as Seedsmen, as we are thus enabled practically to test not only the germinating qualities of all seeds before offering them for sale, but it also enables us to test the claims to merit of new varieties. This we find to be more and more necessary every season, as our "European Novelties" increase in number, and we find that it is folly to expect more than one in a dozen to be worth cultivating.

Those who receive this Catalogue only, may have the Seed Catalogue sent on application. Parties ordering Plants will please make out order on order sheet for Plants; if from Seed Catalogue on order sheet for Seeds, though both can be sent in one order.

Peter Henderson, 35 Cortlandt St., N. Y.

NEW AND SCARCE PLANTS.

A number of these were offered in last year's Catalogue, but our stock being limited of many of them, the prices were such as prevented many from purchasing. All we offered last year, are now offered quite low, and the new varieties this year, which we offer for the first time, are reduced to the lowest rates that our stock will permit of. All plants are *now* ready to ship unless otherwise specified.

ROSES, FIGURED IN COLORED PLATE.

Madame Margottin, yellow and rose.
La Nankin, bright yellow, tipped white.
Madame Capucine, copper yellow, very distinct.
La Phœnix, carmine rose.
Louis Gigot, pure white.
Marie Ducher, deep rose.
Douglas, rich violet, entirely distinct in color.
Madame de St. Joseph, deep pink.
Marie Sisley, white tipped carmine, shell like.
Madame Caroline Kuster, beautiful orange yellow.
Madame Dennis, white, with sulphur yellow centre.
La Jonquille, golden yellow, splendid.

Above are descriptions, but they are probably best described by the colored plate enclosed with this catalogue. This set of twelve Roses are, with three or four exceptions, new varieties, and the whole have been selected as a dozen varieties having the greatest contrast in color, combining at the same time, free flowering qualities, *either for summer or winter blooming.* They are mostly Tea Roses, and are consequently ever-blooming. We have never before sent out any set of plants represented by a colored chromo that we think will be so satisfactory as this set of twelve ever-blooming Roses. We may state, when not wanted for winter flowering, that a covering of six inches of dry leaves or straw aro 1 the roots, put on in December, will preserve them through the winter in the Northern States ; in most of the Southern States they will be hardy without covering.

First size, price $1 50 each, $12 per set of 12 ; second size, price $1 00 each, $9 per set of 12 ; third size, 75 cents each, $6 per set of 12.

Sent by mail when so desired at above rates, but better plants can always be sent by express.

NEW TEA ROSES OF 1873.

Cheshunt Hybrid, purplish maroon, shaded crimson, large and full, growth very vigorous.
Claire Carnot, striking yellow, bordered white and rose; growth vigorous, a new color.
Bignonia, deep orange, of the color of Bignonia grandiflora.
Price $1 50 each ; set of three for $3.

HYBRID PERPETUAL ROSES, (12 finest and most distinct.)

Victor Verdier, rosy carmine.
Anna de Diesbach, clear rose, very large and showy.
Fisher Holmes, reddish scarlet.
Coquette des Blanches, pure white, the best white H. P. yet introduced.
Marquisse de Ligneris, bright rose.
Baron de Bonstetton, violet crimson, richly shaded.
La France, beautiful pale peach, rose centre, free bloomer.
Alfred Colomb, bright fiery red, large and full.
Reine Victoria, brilliant rose.
Bessie Johnson, light blush, very double, fragrant.
President Thiers, bright red.
Rev. H. Dombrain, bright carmine, large and fine.
Price $1 each ; $9 per set of twelve.

HYBRID PERPETUAL ROSE, "Firebrand,"

Of the style of Giant of the Battles ; color, scarlet crimson, double, symetrical in form, fragrant, and entirely hardy. Considered by the raiser, Wm. Paul, to be the finest rose of its class.
Price $1 50 each ; $12 per dozen.

COLEUS, "The Shah," or "Lady Burrill."

We imported the "Shah" Coleus last season, but as it showed no indications of the singular leaf-marking as shown in the engraving above, threw it away, thinking we had got a wrong sort, but on importing it again last summer, we found that on growing it to a large plant, it showed its beautiful markings on every plant, after it had grown to the height of two or three feet. All who now buy it from us again this season, may expect that the young plants they receive may have no indications of the curious leaf-marking, but plain, like the ordinary bronze sorts—at the same time, they may rest assured that the half of each leaf will assume a golden yellow color as soon as the plant is grown. See cut.   50 cents each. $4 50 per dozen.

COLEUS. (Newer Sorts.)

Serrata. Maroon, deeply serrated, and bordered yellow.
Startler. Dark crimson, with maroon centre.
Beppo. Bright golden yellow, centre purplish red.
Belle Lamar. Rich velvet crimson, yellow edge.
Supreme. Bright cinnamon, very broad yellow margin.
Holandi. Crimson maroon, deeply serrated and margined bright yellow.
Nellie Grant. Fine crimson scarlet, broad yellow edge.
50 cents each; $4 50 per dozen. $3 00 for set of eight, including C. "The Shah."

ACHYRANTHES LINDENII AUREA RETICULATA.

A sport from "A. Lindenii" which it resembles in form, the leaves are bright green, netted with yellow, with bright carmine mid-rib, and stems. 50 cents each. $4 50 per dozen.

BOUVARDIA. Lady Hyslop.

This variety is now one of our standard winter blooming sorts, of free vigorous growth, resembling "Elegans," with flowers of a light-rose color. See cut. Price 75 cents each; $6 per dozen.

BOUVARDIA. Bridal Wreath.

An excellent winter blooming variety, producing its delicate blush white flowers, in the greatest profusion, of the style of B. "Jasminoides," but clusters of flowers, more compact, and growth more vigorous. Price 75 cents each; $6 00 per dozen. The two varieties for $1.

MONOCHÆTUM ENSIFERUM.

A small greenhouse shrub, growing about 2 feet in height, blooming in August, and completely covered with its flowers, of a rosy purple color, a splendid plant for pot culture. 50 cents each. $4 50 per dozen.

DAHLIA COCCINEA.

A single-flowering species with deep crimson petals, and bright yellow disc, growing some 2 feet in height. Flowering in profusion from July to November. Price, 50 cents each. $4 50 per dozen.

HYDRANGEA PANICULATA GRANDIFLORA. *(Syn. H. Deutzæfolia.)*

One of the finest hardy shrubs in cultivation—the flowers are formed in large white panicles, or trusses, six inches in length. The shrub grows to a height and breadth of 4 or 5 feet, and as the flowers slightly droop, few plants have the grace and beauty presented by this magnificent shrub—for Cemetery decoration it has no equal. Continues in flower from August to November. See cut.

Price for extra large stock plants, $3 each. 2d size, $2 each. 3d size, $1 each. 4th size, 50 cents each.

HYDRANGEA. Otaksa.

Similar in color of flower to the common "H. Hortensis," but much larger—besides having the quality of flowering when the plants are quite small—plants of only six inches in height, being surmounted with an immense panicle of its rosy carmine flowers. Price, 50 cents each. $4 50 per dozen

RONDELETIA ANOMALA.

This neat little plant should be in every collection; it will bloom when quite small, and continue in bloom all summer, and if lifted and potted, makes a good winter bloom. ing plant.   Flowers bright vermillion.

Price 30 cents each ; $3 per dozen.

RUSSELIA JUNCEA.

A splendid basket plant, of neat slender habit, with very bright scarlet flowers, which are very conspicuous, a color that is scarce in basket plants.

Price 30 cents each ; $3 per dozen.

VERONICA IMPERIALIS.

The Veronicas are a very distinct class of plants, blooming during the fall and winter months. The colors predominating being white, blue or lilac, but in Veronica Imperialis we have an entirely distinct color, an amaranth red, changing as the flower grows older to carmine.   See cut

Price 60 cents each ; $4 50 per dozen.

VERONICA CREME ET VIOLET.

A neat dwarf variety, flowers changing from pale rose to mauve ; a beautiful plant either for planting in the open ground or for pot culture.

Price 60 cents each ; $4 50 per dozen   The two sorts for $1.

ŒNOTHERA SPECIOSA.

A hardy herbaceous plant, having pure white moon-like flowers, 3 inches in diameter, flowering in July and August. It is a very old plant, but it possesses qualities that should guarantee its cultivation in every garden.

Price 50 cents each $4 50 per dozen.

MESEMBRYANTHEMUM CORDIFOLIUM VARIEGATUM.

(Variegated Ice Plant.)

A new plant which we have found to be exceedingly valuable for Baskets or Vases, as its succulent character enables it to stand our hot and dry weather admirably; the variegation of the leaves white and green is very distinct, and the star-like purple flowers contrast finely with the creamy white foliage. This plant is considered one of the finest for front "ribbon lines," and is used in immense quantities in "Battersea Park" and other public grounds about London. We had more difficulty in importing this plant than any thing we ever tried, having imported over 50 plants at six different times before we succeeded in getting one alive; but once got, it is easily grown and propagated. See cut.

Price 50 cents each ; $4 50 per dozen.

FEVERFEW.—New Dwarf.

Quite an improvement on the old double white variety, the flowers are larger and the plant of dwarfer habit.

Price 30 cents each : $3 per dozen.

TRADESCANTIA AQUATICA.

For rock work, margins of fountains, vases or baskets, when placed in the shade this plant is excellently adapted. For a window plant, where a green screen of drooping foliage is desired, it is unequaled. See cut.

Price 30 cents each ; $3 per dozen.

TRADESCANTIA REPENS VITTATA.

A very beautifully marked variety, the leaves of which are bright green, striped with creamy white. A very effective basket plant.

Price 30 cents each ; $3 per dozen.

ABUTILON BOULE DE NIEGE.

This is by far the best white flowering Abutilon that has yet been introduced ; all other white flowering sorts have been coarse growing, but in this variety we find a compact growth and abundance of flowers, well suiting it for house culture, where white flowers are desired in winter. See cut.

Price 50 cents each ; $4 50 per dozen.

FITTONIA, (Gymnostachyum.)

Low growing plants, of creeping habit, grown for the beauty of their leaves, which are veined in the most curious manner with lines of white, carmine and crimson.   Valuable plants for Wardian Cases or Ferneries, or for growing in shaded greenhouses or rooms.

Argyroneura, bright green, netted with silvery white.
Gigantea, coloring like the two following sorts, but of stronger growth.
Pearcii, green, netted with pink and red.
Verschaffelti, reticulated, with red passing into brilliant crimson.

Price 30 cents each ; $3 per dozen.

LATANIA BORBONICA.

This *Palm* is too well known to need any description ; its strong constitution, and other general characteristics render it one of the most easily grown.

Price 50 cents each ; $4 50 per dozen.

NEW PANSY.—"White Treasure."

This valuable new bedding Pansy was raised by a Western Florist, from whom we have this season purchased the stock, and believe it is now offered for sale the first time. Besides the valuable quality of coming true from seed, it is a most abundant bloomer, growing and flowering without intermission during the entire summer and fall months. For decorative purposes in Cemetery grounds, it will be very valuable, as well as for all purposes where white flowers in massing are required. Flowers are large, of the purest white. See cut. Price 50 cents each; $4 50 per dozen.

EUCALYPTUS GLOBULUS, (Blue Gum Tree.)
"The Fever and Ague Plant."

We have grown a few plants of this merely to show to those who are curious in the matter, what it is like, without believing for a moment in its Fever and Ague properties. It grows to a large tree, and is not hardy in northern latitudes. It is, however, rather a pretty tree, and would form an object of interest in sub-tropical planting.
Price 50 cents each; $4 50 per dozen.

DOUBLE BLUE LOBELIA.

One of the novelties of the season, and a most valuable one; in habit it is similar to the compact growing single varieties, but having double flowers somewhat resembling the double Violet. Like all plants having double flowers, its duration of blooming is much longer, and whether this valuable plant is used for baskets, or for bedding in the open ground, it will prove a valuable acquisition. It has been introduced in England over a year, but its great difficulty in importation prevented it being got here alive last season. See colored plate.
Price 75 cents each; $7 50 per dozen.

OTHONNA CRASSIFOLIA.

Not a new plant, but now scarce. In habit it somewhat resembles some of our varieties of Sedums It is excellently adapted for carpeting the ground under shrubs, or as a plant for baskets or vases. It has small bright-yellow tassel-like flowers, which are borne in great profusion.   Price 50 cents each. $4 50 per dozen.

SALVIA ROSEA.

A distinct winter-flowering Salvia, with rich rose-colored flowers, borne in spikes, six inches in length—to contrast with the white, blue and scarlet varieties of Salvia, it is very valuable.   Price 50 cents each. $4 50 per dozen.

SAXIFRAGA JAPONICA TRICOLOR.

This resembles the old variety, "Sarmentosa" in habit, with leaves irregularly variegated with crimson, bronze, and white. A splendid basket plant. $1 each.

FUCHSIA "Sunray."

One of the most beautiful ornamental-leaved varieties ever introduced. Its colors much resemble that of the well-known Geranium "Mrs. Pollock." Flowers violet and crimson.   Price $1 50 each.

FUCHSIAS. Newer Sorts of 1873 and 1874.

Standard. Sepals very broad, about 2 inches long, of a rich cherry pink, corolla rich violet purple.
Leah. Tube and sepals white, corolla rich purplish crimson.
Beacon. Sepals deep rose, deep carmine corolla shaded with violet.
Dictator. Bright red sepals, completely reflexed, corolla violet plum color.
Monah. Rich crimson sepals, deep purple corolla, very full and double.
Lillah. Reflexed sepals, of a rich crimson color, corolla satiny purple.
Victoria. Sepals red, corolla extra large, double flowered, purplish blue.
La Neige. Corolla white, carmine sepals.
Little Gem. Glossy pink sepals, fine cobalt blue corolla.
Canary Bird. Foliage bright yellow, sepals scarlet, well reflexed, corolla dark purple.
Theresa. Sepals creamy white, ruby red corolla.
Climax. Bright red sepals, white corolla.
Price, 75 cents each.   Per set of 12, $6 00.

NEW VERBENAS.

Maud. Large, pink, yellow eye.	**Mariana.** Rosy carmine, yellow eye.
Neptune. Light lilac.	**Arab.** Large purple magenta.
Willie. Violet crimson, yellow centre.	**Yeddo.** Pinkish salmon, white eye.
Nemesis. Brilliant scarlet, yellow eye.	**Ernani.** Large purplish plum color.
Waterloo. Crimson, maroon centre.	**Eureka.** Beautiful cerise pink.
Claudius. Large, bright cherry, sulphur eye.	**Negro.** Black, extra fine.
Haidee. Violet maroon, lilac eye.	**Coggia.** Large dazzling scarlet, yellow eye.
Evangeline. Clear pink, shaded rose.	**Regent.** Deep claret, violet eye.
Lara. Purplish crimson, lemon eye.	**Niobe.** Large, pure white.
Torch. Brilliant scarlet, yellow eye.	**Lulu.** Pure white, splashed with salmon.
Gertrude. Large, magenta rose.	**Mozart.** Splashed scarlet and white.
Sonnet. Scarlet, large white eye.	**Cremona.** Rich crimson, bordered purple.
Lepante. Ruby crimson, yellow eye.	**Manifred.** Bright carmine, yellow eye.
Bonfire. Large, vermilion, yellow centre.	**Garnet.** Blood red violet eye.
Adrian. Carmine, purple eye.	**Domingo.** Dark crimson maroon.

Price 30 cents each; $3.00 per dozen; per set of 30, $6.00.
For general collection, see body of catalogue.

PELARGONIUMS. (Newer Sorts.)

No description of Pelargoniums can ever properly convey to the reader what they are; we merely say in general terms that few plants grown excel in brilliancy of coloring the flowers of this class, ranging through all the shades of white, crimson, scarlet, rose, violet, &c., shaded and striped in the different varieties.

Witch.	Glow-worm.
Demosthenes.	Orientale.
Lothair.	Sunrise.
Coquette de Plessis.	Lady Dorothy Neville.
Bianca.	Early Market.
Lady of the Lake,	Prince of Pelargoniums.
Belle of the Ball.	Striped Desdemona.

Price 75 cents each. $7 50 per set of 15; including "Pel. Emperor."   For general collection, see body of Catalogue.

PELARGONIUM "Emperor."

A large fringed flowered Pelargonium, with an invariable tendency to form buds after the French Hybrid Style. The flowers are large, of fine form, the upper petals dark maroon, the lower ones white, shading to scarlet crimson; the petals are elegantly fringed or crisped; a profuse bloomer, dwarf, and one of the best for Florist's use, for forcing.

Price 75 cents each. $6 00 per dozen.

NEW DOUBLE TUBEROSE, "Pearl."

This sort was first sent out by us a few years ago. We have, this season, propagated it largely, so that we can offer it at moderate prices. Its value over the common variety consists in its flowers being of double the size, imbricated like a rose, and its dwarf habit, growing only from 18 inches to 2 feet in height; in other respects it is the same as the common sort. See cut.

Price 30 cents each; $3 per dozen; $18 per 100.

BRONZE GERANIUM, "Black Douglas."

Similar in marking to "Marshal McMahon," but with pink flowers.

Price 75 cents each; $6 per dozen.

BRONZE GERANIUM, "Constantine."

Bronze, with a nearly black ring in the centre of the leaf; flowers carmine.

Price 75 cents each; $6 per dozen. The 8 varieties of Bronze Geraniums for $2.

BRONZE GERANIUM, "Marshal McMahon."

The finest of a dozen of the best new sorts we imported a year ago; ground color of the leaves golden yellow, marked with a deep chocolate ring. Really a grand variety. No variegated Geranium of its class yet equals it; flowers scarlet.

Price 75 cents each; $6 per dozen.

NEW SILVER-LEAVED GERANIUM, "Avalanche."

One of the whitest leaved sorts of vigorous growth, with pure white flowers, making it valuable for massing where a white group or line is required. See cut.

Price $1 each.

SCENTED GERANIUM, "Filicifolia."

A very distinct fern-like leaved variety, particularly useful for mixing with cut flowers.

Price 75 cents each; $6 per dozen.

NEW IVY GERANIUM, "Dolly Varden."

This is a Bronze Ivy leaved Geranium, the first of its class. The leaf is of a rich golden tint, with a bronze zone, the older leaves becoming tinted red at the margin. It is of vigorous growth, of compact habit, with flowers of bright pink.

Price $1 each.

NEW IVY GERANIUM, "Alice Lee."

Leaf golden yellow, flowers violet crimson—growth free and dense.

Price $1 each.

DOUBLE GERANIUM, "Admiration."

This is, without doubt, the best pink double Geranium yet introduced, as a trial with all the standard varieties of previous years has proved to us the past season. In color it is much darker than "Madame Lemoine," more dwarf, with trusses larger, and blooming as freely as any of the single sorts.

Price 50 cents each; $4 50 per dozen.

DOUBLE GERANIUM, "Asa Gray."

Quite a new color in double Geraniums—a distinct shade of salmon pink; it also, like the preceding, blooms as profusely as the single sorts,

Price 50 cents each; $4 50 per dozen.

DOUBLE GERANIUM, "Le Negre."

The darkest in color of all the class; a rich purplish crimson, double as a rose, large compact truss, and like the others above named, of free blooming qualities. This was one of the scarcest sorts of last season, and was sold at $2 per plant.

Price 50 cents each; $4 50 per dozen.

DOUBLE GERANIUM, "Aline Sisley."

The best of the double *whites;* although only half double, we found that last season this variety improved upon farther acquaintance, as for "bedding" purposes it bloomed as profusely as the single whites, while its double property enabled the flowers to remain a long time without dropping, and also from the same cause, like all the double Geraniums, it is very useful for cut flowers, while the single varieties of all kinds are worthless for that purpose.

Price 50 cents each; $4 50 per dozen.

DOUBLE GERANIUM, "La Promise."

The largest and most perfect of all the scarlet doubles we have seen; single flowers measure nearly an inch in diameter, perfectly double, and of the most vivid scarlet.

Price 50 cents each; $4 50 per dozen.

The above FIVE sorts of Double Geraniums, in our opinion, combine the greatest contrast of color, with the best blooming qualities.

Price per set of five sorts, $2.

NEW DOUBLE GERANIUM, "Jewell."

A very dwarf variety, a free bloomer, with trusses of good size, deep scarlet in color; each separate flower is regularly formed, resembling a miniature Rose. The foliage is slightly zoned, and is not as coarse as double Geraniums usually are. See cut.

Price $1 each.

APPLE SCENTED GERANIUM.

The Apple Scented Geranium is usually more scarce than any of the scented varieties, from the fact that its manner of growth is such that it never makes good plants when grown from cuttings, and must be grown from seed to produce good plants. Our plants this season are particularly fine.

Large size, 50 cents each, $4 50 per dozen. Second size, 30 cents each, $3 per dozen.

NEW CARNATION, "La Belle."

One of the new so called "climbing" class of Carnations ; flowers rather small, double white, although from its slender habit of growth it is easily trained in the manner shown in the cut ; it must be tied to the stakes, as it does not adhere of itself, as the word climb might indicate. See cut.

Price 50 cents each ; $4 50 per dozen.

NEW CARNATION, "Peerless."

Pure white, fine form, a splendid winter flowering sort, flowers often two inches in diameter.

Price 50 cents each ; $4 50 per dozen.

NEW CARNATION, "Mrs. McKenzie."

Color light rose, perfect form, flowering abundantly during winter and spring, having an exquisite clove fragrance.

Price 50 cents each ; $4 50 per dozen.

NEW CARNATIONS---Zeller's Collection.

Prince of Wales, scarlet, of the "climbing" class.
George Washington, white ground, striped and dotted cherry red.
Admiral Dupont, carmine, fine bloomer.
Monsieur Gambetta, yellow ground, flaked crimson.
Horace Greeley, slate, flaked bright red, free grower and profuse bloomer.
Indispensable, deep yellow, feathered and flaked bright red.
H. W. Beecher, white ground, flaked and striped violet, maroon and carmine.
Isabella Barnum, salmon, flaked crimson.
President McMahon, fiery red, flaked dark maroon.

Price of the above $1 each, or full collection of 12 new sorts for $7 50.

NEW CHRYSANTHEMUMS.

Monsieur de Soulages, cherry pink.
Baron D'Ulimbert, a splendid flower, rich dark violet purple.
Solomon, orange and cinnamon, very dwarf.
Rosabella, carmine and white.
Donna Carnea, white.

Price 50 cents each ; $2 for set of five.

KLENIA REPENS.

A succulent plant with long fleshy glaucus, upright, green leaves used as a basket plant or for bedding with other succulents.

Price 30 cents each ; $3 per dozen.

EUPHORBIA SPLENDENS.

A continuous blooming variety, densely covered on the stems with spines an inch in length, giving it a curious appearance; bright scarlet flowers, with a yellow centre, of great value for bouquets.

Price 50 cents each ; $4 50 per dozen. Larger plants $1 each

CENTRADENIA GRANDIFLORA.

An upright growing plant with narrow leaves, the under side of which are crimson ; profusely covered with small pink flowers during most of the year. Excellent for baskets, ferneries, &c.

Price 50 cents each ; $4 50 per dozen.

BEGONIA GLAUCOPHYLLA SCANDENS.

A drooping or creeping species, with large panicles of orange salmon flowers: grown in hanging baskets it is one of the most beautiful plants in cultivation. See cut.
Price 75 cents each; $7 50 per dozen.

BEGONIAS---Mostly New Sorts.

Degswelliana, bright scarlet.
Subpeltata Nigricans, large ornamental leaves, flowers produced very freely.
Sutherlandii, a tuberous rooted sort, flowers yellow, very distinct.
Parnelli, leaves beautifully spotted with silvery white, on a dark green back ground.
Price 75 cents each; set of five, including "Begonia Glaucophylla Scandens," $3.

PLUMBAGO ALBA AND ROSEA.

Two rather scarce and beautiful plants, valued for their free flowering. Plants when only a few inches in height blooming abundantly during the summer and winter. The first is white, and the second rose color.
Price 50 cents each; $4 50 per dozen.

GRAPTOPHYLLUM PICTUM

Or "Caricature Plant," so called from its resemblance in the outline of variegation to the human face; the leaves are dark glossy green, with a well-defined yellow blotch in the centre of each. See cut.

Price $1 each ; $9 per dozen.

FRAGARIA INDICA. (Indian Strawberry.)

A "Strawberry" producing bright scarlet berries, that remain on the plant for a long time. It is a beautiful plant for baskets, the runners hanging down on the sides, giving a very graceful effect. The fruit is not fit to eat, but is highly ornamental, particularly when grown in baskets.

Price 30 cents each : $3 per dozen.

HABROTHAMUS COCCINEUS.

A bright scarlet variety of this valuable winter flowering plant, bearing a profusion of bright scarlet tassel-like flowers ; valuable for forcing.

Price 50 cents each ; $4 50 per dozen.

GLAUCIUM CORNICULATUM.

A white leaved ornamental plant with long silvery-white velvety leaves, gracefully recurved, deeply cut to the mid-rib, and each leaf again cut and curled ; the flowers are orange yellow, bell shaped, and drooping. It is of vigorous growth ; its silvery color makes a fine contrast with dark colored foliage plants.

Price 30 cents each ; $3 per dozen.

VARIEGATED ALTHEA. (Rose of Sharon.)

A variegated leaved variety of this popular shrub, with the leaves distinctly margined with pure white.

Price 50 cents each ; $4 50 per dozen.

HIBISCUS SINENSIS VERSICOLOR.

A variety combining in its flowers all the colors of the whole family, being handsomely striped, crimson, buff, rose and white; the flowers average from 3 to 4 inches in diameter, and are borne just as freely as in the common variety.

Price 60 cents each ; $6 per dozen.

HIBISCUS SINENSIS GRANDIFLORÆ.

An improvement on Hibiscus Sinensis, which it resembles in habit, with much larger flowers of a rosy crimson, with a distinct black spot in the centre of each flower. The "Hibiscus" are equally good both for summer or winter blooming. See cut.
Price 60 cents each; $6 per dozen. The two sorts for $1.

BLETIA TANKERVILLIÆ.

A terrestrial orchid of easy culture, the flowers of which, as in all of the orchid family, are of great beauty. They are borne in spikes, on stems, about 18 inches high; the color of the flowers is white, marked with brown, but a mere description can hardly convey an adequate idea of their beauty.
Strong plants $2 each.

PHYSIANTHUS ALBENS.

A beautiful climber, flowering during the summer and fall months. It is of rapid growth; the flowers are pure white, exceedingly useful for summer bouquets; the seed pods are as large as an orange and are very ornamental.

Price 50 cents each; $4 50 per dozen.

WISTARIA SINENSIS---Var. Allenii.

A new variety of this well-known hardy climber, differing from the old variety in having darker flowers, which are developed with the leaves. The fault in the common sort being that the flowers were produced before the leaves. To those who do not know the Wistaria, we will say that it is perhaps the most magnificent of all hardy climbing plants, climbing to a height of fifty feet or more, loaded to profusion with its racemes of purple flowers, resembling in size and shape a bunch of grapes. This new sort, we believe, will prove a valuable addition.

Price $1 each; $9 per dozen.

DIANTHUS QUERTERI (German Pink.)

This beautiful Pink we imported some five years ago, but it is yet very scarce. Few plants we cultivate possess so many points of excellence; it grows to the height of a foot, flowers rich purplish crimson, two inches in diameter, double and well-formed; it blooms without intermission from June to January, and is an exceedingly useful plant for bouquets; clove scented. See cut.

Price 30 cents each; $3 per dozen.

POLYGONUM SCANDENS.

A trailing or creeping plant, suitable either for baskets or vases. The leaves are small, round, bright green, and keep the foliage well in the parlor or sitting room in winter doing well in the shade.

Price 50 cents each; $4 50 per dozen.

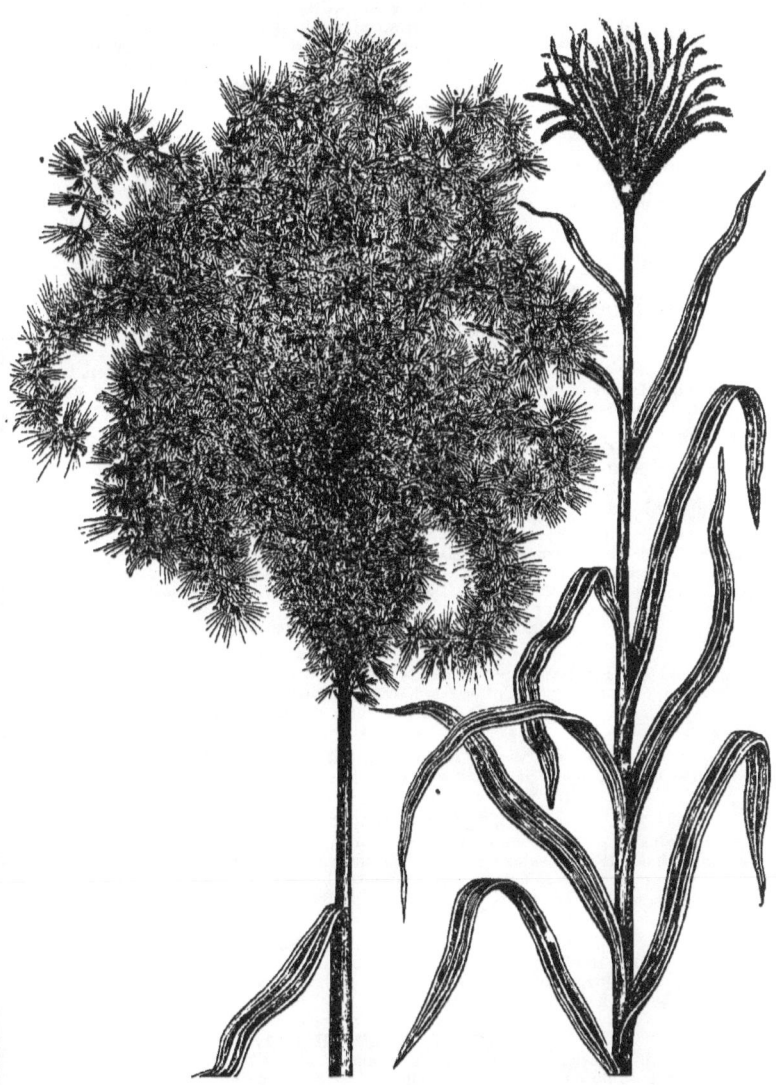

EULALIA JAPONICA VAR.

Incorrectly given in some catalogues as "Imperata Japonica." It is an entirely new and distinct ornamental grass, of easy culture, and perfectly hardy. It has long narrow leaves striped white and green, throwing up stalks from four to six feet in height, terminated with a cluster of flower spikes on which the individual flowers are arranged; the flowers are surrounded by long silky threads, which, when fully ripe or when placed in a warm room expand, giving the whole head a most graceful and beautiful appearance, not unlike that of an ostrich feather when curled. These dry flowers will be valuable as parlor ornaments, as they retain their beauty for a long time. See cut.

Price $1 each; 9 per dozen.

MIKANIA VIOLACEA.

A climbing or creeping plant, with very striking foliage of a purplish green—with a velvet-like upper surface, under glossy carmine; though not a new plant, it is quite scarce, having been only recently introduced here. It will be a most desirable plant f r baskets, the color of the leaves being novel and different from anything else we have been using for that purpose; it grows and roots freely.

Price 50 cents each ; $4 50 per dozen.

SOLLYA HETEROPHYLLA.

A beautiful summer climbing plant, with bright blue flowers, growing to the height of six feet, well adapted for covering trellis work where a neat, handsome climber is desired. It is quite an old plant but now scarce.

Price 50 cents each ; $4 50 per dozen.

ASPIDISTRA LURIDA.

Curious plants, remarkable for producing their flowers under the surface of the earth. The leaves are six inches long, about two inches wide, and of a bright green, well adapted for wardian cases, ferneries, &c.

Price 50 cents each ; $4 50 per dozen.

POLYGONUM FILIFORME FOL. VAR.

A hardy herbaceous plant, the leaves of which are variegated white and green, bearing rosy pink flowers in long racemes, which droop over the foliage, giving a very pleasing effect. It grows to the height of two feet.

Price 75 cents each ; $7 50 per dozen.

PEDILANTHUS PADIFOLIUS, (Slipper Plant.)

A curious plant, resembling the "Euphorbia" in habit and general appearance.

Price 50 cents each ; $4 50 per dozen.

HEBECLINUM MACROPHYLLUM.

Not new, but of recent introduction here ; it is of the class of "Ageratum" or "Eupatorium," having white flowers, borne on large trusses during January and February. It is a free vigorous growing plant, and will be valued as an addition to our winter flowering plants, filling in the gap of this class of white flowers, which is left by most of the others blooming either too early or too late.

Price 50 cents each ; $4 50 per dozen.

CYPERUS ALTERNIFOLIUS.

A grass-like plant, throwing up stems to the height of about two feet, surmounted at the top by a cluster or whorl of leaves, diverging horizontally, giving the plant a very curious appearance. A splendid plant for the centre of baskets, vases, or wardian cases, or as a water plant.   Price 50 cents each : $4 50 per dozen.

CYPERUS ALTERNIFOLIUS VARIEGATUS.

Similar to the above in habit, but striped with white.

Price $1 each ; $9 per dozen.

CRASSULA CORDATA.

An invaluable plant for winter blooming, and one that should command more attention than it has. It blooms during the late fall months and holidays. It is very prolific in its bloom, small plants in four inch pots often sending up five or six spikes of pinkish white star shaped flowers, lasting a long time in perfection.

Price 30 cents each ; $3 per dozen.

CRASSULA LACTEA, (Syn. Perfoliata.)

This, like the preceding, is a valuable winter blooming plant, but of dwarfer and denser growth. The flowers are pure white, star shaped, and produced on plants when quite young. It blooms just before Christmas, and is a favorite with the bouquet makers.

Price 50 cents each ; $4 per dozen.

CRASSULA SPATHULATA.

A low trailing succulent plant, with heart shaped leaves, bearing clusters of small white star shaped flowers. It is valuable for rock work, baskets or vases.

Price 30 cents each ; $3 per dozen.

CEREUS, (Night Blooming Cactus.)

Triangularis, stems triangular, flowers white.
Grandiflorus, true night blooming cactus, straw color.
Nycticallis, yellowish white.

Price 50 cents each ; the 8 sorts for $1.

COWSLIP, (Primula Veris.)

A favorite early free flowering plant, very useful for filling the beds and borders in early spring ; flowers red and yellow, perfectly hardy.

Price 25 cents each ; $2 25 per dozen.

GENERAL COLLECTION.

(Alphabetical Arrangement.)

ABUTILONS.

Greenhouse shrubs, growing from two to six feet in height; flowers pendulous, bell-shaped; blooming in abundance during the winter and spring months.

Mesopamicum, flowers scarlet and yellow, low habit.
Mesopamicum Var., leaves variegated yellow and green.
Santana, flowers brownish crimson.
    "   **Alba,** flowers large white.
Duc de Malakoff, flowers large crimson, veined.
Thompsonii, leaves mottled or marked with bright golden yellow.
    Price 30 cents each ; $3 per dozen. Set of 6 sorts for $1 50.

ALTERNANTHERAS.

A genus of plants growing from six to twelve inches in height, of the class known as ornamental foliaged plants, to which their beautiful leaf tints well entitle them. Well adapted for baskets, vases, or ribbon lines.

Parychoides, leaves tinted green, crimson and straw color.
    "   **Major,** leaves carmine, yellow and green.
Spectabile, leaves orange, bronze and scarlet.
Spathulata, leaves tinted carmine and green.
Versicolor, leaves tinted light rose to deep crimson.
Amœna, leaves yellow, brown and rose. Very fine.
Magnifica, leaves broad, yellow, scarlet and green.
Latifolia, broad, smooth, autumn tinted leaves.
    Price 25 cents each ; $2 25 per dozen. Set of 8 sorts for $1 50.

ACHYRANTHES.

Bright leaved plants, used largely in ribbon gardening and massing, for which they are admirably adapted from their easy culture, standing the hottest summer weather, and keeping their bright-hued tints until destroyed by frost.

Aurea Reticulata, leaves bright green, marked with a net work of bright yellow.
Gilsonii, au improvement on "A. Verschaffeltii;" leaves carmine, stems a rich shade of pink.
Lindenii, deep blood red, changing to crimson, leaves lanceolate.
Lindenii Aurea Reticulata. Price 50 cents. See novelties.
    Price 25 cents each ; $2 25 per dozen, except where noted. $1 for set of 4.

AGERATUM.

Old garden favorites, blooming continually through the summer months, and making excellent winter blooming plants; for this reason they are peculiarly adapted for bouquets, baskets of cut flowers, &c.; of the easiest culture.

White Tom Thumb, dwarf, growing not more than six inches in height, profusely covered with bluish white flowers.
Blue Tom Thumb, habit the same as the preceding, with flowers of a beautiful light porcelain blue.
Imperial Dwarf, a variety of "A. Mexicanum," which it resembles; flowers blue.
Mexicanum, flowers light blue.
Mexicanum Var., leaves variegated with creamy white, flowers blue, a valuable addition to our var. plants.
Mexicanum Nanum, a dwarf var. of "A. Mexicanum."
Prince Alfred, a newer variety, habit medium, with flowers of a delicate lilac shade.
Lasseauxii, a complete novelty in color, being of a rose or pink shade, blooming all summer.
    Price 25 cents each ; $2 25 per dozen. 8 sorts for $1 50.

AKEBIA QUINATA.

A beautiful hardy evergreen climber, attaining a height of twenty feet; flowers dark brown, and deliciously fragrant. One of the most valuable climbing plants.
Price 30 cents each; $3 per dozen.

ALOYSIA CITRIODORA. (Lemon Verbena.)

Of this well-known shrub, so indispensable for the delightful fragrance of its leaves, in the construction of bouquets, &c., we offer very fine bushy plants.
Price 25 cents each; $2 25 per dozen; $15 per hundred.
Extra sized plants, double rates.

ANEMONE JAPONICA, ALBA AND RUBRA.

One of the most beautiful of our hardy herbaceous plants. The plant attains a height of two feet, flowering in profusion from August to November; two varieties, white and red. See cut.   Price 30 cents each; $3 per dozen.

AMPELOPSIS VEITCHII. (A. Tricuspidata.)

A miniature variety of the Virginia creeper, the young growth during summer is a dark purple, changing in fall to the brightest tints of scarlet, crimson and orange. It clings to stone work, trees, &c., and is a splendid plant for covering unsightly objects, &c.; it attains a height of fifty feet.
Price 30 cents each; $3 per dozen.

AMPELOPSIS TRICOLOR.

A variety, the young growth of which is elegantly variegated with white, pink and green, a perfectly hardy variety, growing to the tops of the highest trees.
Price 30 cents each; $3 per dozen.

AMPELOPSIS QUINQUEFOLIA.

This is the well-known Virginia creeper, found in many parts of the country; it is a fast grower, of strong habit, and is splendidly variegated in the fall.
Price 25 cents each; $2 25 per dozen.

ASTILBE JAPONICA, (Spirea Japonica.)

One of the finest of hardy garden plants; when in flower it is about one foot in height. The flowers are borne in branching feather-like spikes of purest white. It is used extensively for forcing for flowers by the bouquet makers. See cut.
Price for extra large clumps, 50 cents each; $4 50 per dozen.
" " smaller " 30 " " 3 00 "

ANTIRRHINUMS.

We offer, this year, an unusually fine lot of Antirrhinums, seedlings, from seed saved from the finest and most beautifully flaked, mottled and striped varieties in cultivation.
Price 25 cents each; $2 25 per dozen.

AZALEA INDICA.

Twelve of the most distinct and beautiful varieties.
Price 50 cents each; $4 50 per dozen.

ARTEMISIA ARGENTEA.

A finely cut, silvery leaved plant, the leaves having an agreeable odor. Well adapted for baskets.

Price 25 cents each ; $2 25 per dozen.

ARTEMISIA STELLARIANA.

An old plant, which has been brought into cultivation now, in consequence of the great demand for plants with white foliage, for hanging baskets, ribbon-lines, &c. The foliage is of the silvery shade of the Centaureas, but as it grows much freer, and is more easily propagated than these, it will soon become popular, as it can be sold at cheaper rates.

Price 25 cents each ; $2 25 per dozen ; $15 per hundred.

AJUGA REPTANS.

An old herbaceous plant, that the modern style of massing in colored foliage has brought into notice. It contrasts markedly with any light foliaged plant of low growth, as its leaves are of dark chocolate color ; almost black.

Price 30 cents each ; $3 per dozen.

ACHIMENES.

We have a large assortment of these beautiful summer blooming plants, embracing a large variety ; colors violet, pink, white, yellow, &c., very suitable for baskets.

Price 50 cents each ; $4 50 per dozen.

BALMS, VARIEGATED.

Pretty hardy perennials ; the leaves emitting an agreeable and refreshing fragrance ; they are of the easiest culture, and luxuriate in the shade, and are thus particularly suited for shrubbery or for city gardens.

Golden leaved, price 25 cents each , $2 25 per dozen ; $15 per hundred.
Silver   "   " 25   "   " 2 25   "   15   "

BOUVARDIA ELEGANS.

Originated in 1868. A sport from **B. Hogarth**, which it resembles in color, only the shade is brighter and clearer, and may be described as a light scarlet carmine, but its extraordinary novelty and merit consists in its immense size of flower and truss, which far exceeds that of any other known variety, many of the trusses measuring from four to five inches in diameter. One of the most valuable of our winter-flowering plants.

Large strong roots, 30 cents each ; $3 per dozen.

BOUVARDIAS---In Variety.

These are now among the most important plants cultivated for winter flowers, owing to the yearly increasing variety of color, and excellent adaptation for that purpose. They are also effective as bedding plants for the flower garden, beginning to bloom in August, and continuing until frost.

Elegans, bright carmine.
Vreelandii, white.
Leiantha, dark, dazzling scarlet.
Jasminoides, pure white, fragrant.
Davidsonii, white, fine form.

Price 30 cents each ; $3 per dozen.

BELLIS PERENNIS, (Daisy.)

One of the prettiest spring flowers—of colors varying through all the shades of white, pink and carmine ; they can be either grown from seeds or by divisions of the roots : in flower from April to June.

Price 15 cents each ; $1 50 per dozen.

BRYOPHYLLUM CALYCINUM.

A species of house leek, growing very rapidly ; the leaves have the peculiarity, if placed in a damp situation, of striking root at the edges, and sending up innumerable small plants. They will occasionally do this when on the plant during very wet summer weather. This singular property of itself makes it a plant of much interest.

Price 25 cents each ; $2 25 per dozen.

BEGONIA HYBRIDA MULTIFLORA.

BEGONIAS.

These are now among our principal winter flowering plants, flowers hanging in graceful panicles of the various colors given in descriptions below. They require rather a warm atmosphere in winter, an average of 70 degrees. See cut.

Robusta, flowers bright carmine, large panicles.
Nitida Alba, flowers white. "
Weltoniensis, flowers rich shade of pink.
Fuchsoides Alba, flowers pure white, *finest winter sort.*
Argyrostygma Veitchi, flowers pink, leaves spotted white.
Saundersonii, flowers of bright scarlet crimson.
Hybrida Multiflora, small ornamental leaves, rosy pink flowers. See cut.
Parviflora, flowers white, neat habit.
Nitida, flowers light flesh color.
Alba, flowers pure white, produced very freely.
Foliosa, white, with neat drooping foliage, good for baskets.
Richardsonii, flowers pure white, in large panicles.

Price 30 cents each; $3 per dozen.

BEGONIA REX---Ornamental Leaved.

Six varieties—50 cents each, $2 50 per set.

CALLA ETHIOPACA.

A fine house plant, sometimes known as the "Lily of the Nile." It requires an abundance of water during the growing season, and should have a period of rest during May and June by turning the pots on their sides in some shady place.

Price 30 cents each; $3 per dozen.

CALLA ETHIOPICA NANA. (Dwarf Ethiopian Lily.)

A dwarf variety, smaller in all its parts than the original. In this respect it is more desirable, being more convenient to handle than the strong-growing variety ; the flowers also being much smaller, can be used to greater advantage in vases and baskets of cut flowers.

Price 50 cents each ; $4 50 per dozen.

CAMELLIA JAPONICA.

Twelve of the best and most distinct sorts.

Price $1 each ; $9 per dozen.

COCCOLOBA PLATYCLADA.

A curious flat stemmed plant, growing to the height of two feet, bearing its small whitish flowers at the axils of the stems, having no leaves, the stems answering in their stead, thus resembling the cactus.

Price 30 cents each ; $3 per dozen.

CORONILLA GLAUCA.

There are very few really good yellow blooming plants that will answer either for summer or winter blooming   This is one of the best, bearing bright yellow pea shaped flowers, which are very fragrant.

Price 30 cents each ; $3 per dozen.

CANNA INDICA---in Variety.

Plants grown mainly for their rich foliage, though having also the advantage of additional beauty in their flowers, varying in many shades of crimson, scarlet, orange and yellow.   12 named sorts ; mostly new dark leaved varieties.

Price 30 cents each ; $3 per dozen.

CALADIUMS---in Variety.

We this year offer the superb collection of Caladiums, seen by many of our customers last season in our greenhouses. To attempt descriptions of the wonderful markings of the leaves of this beautiful tribe would be only confusing. Suffice it to say that they assume almost every imaginable color in their variegation of spotting, veining, and marbling of the leaves ; the cut represents **Argyrites**, a beautiful white spotted variety, one of the smallest growing kinds, but many of the other sorts are finer than this.

Price 75 cents each ; $6 per dozen ; collection of 24 sorts for $10 50.

licio

Our
Carnatio.
are very l

9 for

white

ts.

. fimbri-

ped.

CHINESE CHRYSANTHEMUMS.---Large-flowering.

Hundreds of our customers have not seen the finer varieties of Chrysanthemums; to such we would say that there is no plant we cultivate, with the exception perhaps, of the Dahlia, that assumes such an extended variety of colors. We have reduced our collection considerably of both large and small flowering kinds. Our list comprises the best and most distinct of the many hundreds we have been cultivating. The Chrysanthemum, being entirely hardy, and of free growth, can be grown on almost any soil and situation with but little care. They are also valuable grown in pots as green-house or parlor plants during the early fall and winter months. The above cut is an excellent representation of this type or class, which we can furnish of any color named below.

Albert Helyer, purplish carmine.	**Large Yellow**, very bright.
Carnation, crimson and white.	**Eve**, white, yellow centre.
Competition, white.	**Mrs. Campbell**, rich crimson.
Countess of Granville, pure white, large.	**Mrs. Keynes**, transparent blush.
Countess of Warwick, sulphur white.	**Prince Alfred**, carmine extra.
Dr. Brook, cinnamon, gold tip.	**Prince of Wales**, purple violet, white centre
Empress of India, clear white.	**Queen of Lilacs**, white and lilac.
Gloria Mundi, brilliant yellow.	**Robert James**, cinnamon and orange,
Grandiflorum, deep yellow.	broad petals.
Hermione, orange, crimson tip.	**Snowball**, pure white, globe shape.
Iona, bright citron yellow.	**Sparkler**, red tinted orange.
Lady Fussell, blush gold tint.	**Temple of Solomon**, deep yellow.
Le Grand, petals broad, rosy peach.	**Venice**, delicate peach shade.
Lucinda, pink, white tip.	**Venus**, lilac peach, large and beautiful.
Minerva, lilac shaded.	**Virgin Queen**, snow white.
Golden Queen, bright yellow.	**Mrs. G. Rundless**, white.

Price 30 cents each; $3 per doz. Set of 30 sorts $6 50, or full collection of 90 sorts for $15.

CUPHEA PLATYCENTRA. (Cigar Plant.)

The tube of the flower is scarlet, with the end part white and crimson, having somewhat the appearance of a miniature lighted cigar.

Price 25 cents each; $2 25 per dozen.

CENTAUREA CANDIDA.

A valuable plant to contrast with Coleus. Leaves downy white, forming a neat compact bush. Massed either with Coleus or Achyranthes, or both, it produces a most pleasing effect.   Price 50 cents each ; $4 50 per dozen.

CENTAUREA GYMNOCARPA.

Attains a diameter of two feet, forming a graceful rounded bush of silvery grey, for which nothing is so well fitted to contrast in ribbon lines with dark foliaged plants. As a plant for hanging baskets it is also unsurpassed, its drooping fern-like leaves being very effective.   Price 30 cents each ; $3 per dozen.

CHOROZEMA VARIA.

An old greenhouse shrub, flowering in winter and spring ; flowers purple and orange, in spikes from 4 to 6 inches in length.
Fine healthy plants, 50 cents each ; $4 50 per dozen.

CINERARIA MARITIMA.

A white foliaged plant, somewhat similar to the Centaurea, but with leaves deeply cut and of more vigorous growth. It is much easier of propagation, and we are therefore enabled to sell it at much lower rates.
Price 25 cents each ; $2 25 per dozen.

CINERARIA ACANTHIFOLIA AND ASPLENÆFOLIA.

Most beautiful white foliaged plants, a little in the style of "C. Maritima," but with wider and longer leaves, and hence more effective, either as specimen plants, or when grown in ribbon-lines. Habit of plants dwarf and stiff.
Price 30 cents each ; $3 per dozen. Set of 3 sorts for 75 cents.

CINERARIA. ("Garden Varieties.")

This is the winter or spring flowering species, hybrids of which are among the most gorgeous of our greenhouse plants; the colors range through all the shades of blue, violet, crimson, pink, maroon and white.
Price 30 cents each ; $3 per dozen.

CLERODENDRON BALFOURII.

A stove climber of great beauty. The flowers, which are of a bright scarlet, are encased by a bag-like calyx of pure white; the trusses or panicles of flowers are upwards of six inches in width, and when trained upon trellises, and hanging down, have a rich and elegant appearance. Although a climber, it may be grown as an ordinary shrubby plant in a pot, it being susceptible of being trained in any way. It is continually in bloom, although more profusely during the winter months, when it may be used as a variety in the formation of bouquets, &c.

Price 50 cents each ; $4 50 per dozen.

CERASTIUM TOMENTOSUM.

Another white-foliaged plant, with small narrow leaves, well suited for hanging baskets or stands; of a trailing or drooping habit; excellent for the front line in ribbon planting.

Price 25 cents each ; $2 25 per dozen.

CESTRUM. (Night Blooming Jessamine.)

C. Aurantiacum, orange flowers, very fragrant.
C. Laurifolium, pure white, very fragrant.

Price 30 cents each ; $3 per dozen. 2 varieties, 50 cents.

CENTRANTHUS RUBER AND ALBO. (Valerian.)

Sometimes called "Garden Heliotrope." Hardy plants, well adapted for summer cut flowers, forming graceful spikes of red and white.

Price 30 cents each ; $3 per dozen.

CISSUS LINDENII.

A stove climber, with large heart shaped leaves, with silvery markings on a clear green ground.

Price 30 cents each; $3 per dozen.

CISSUS AMAZONICA.

Similar habit to the above, the under sides of the leaves are bright crimson; the upper side bluish green: a very ornamental variety.

Price 30 cents each; $3 per dozen.

CISSUS DISCOLOR.

A well-known stove climber, with leaves beautifully shaded with dark green, purple and white, the upper surface of the leaf having a rich, velvet-like appearance. The leaves are much used in New York for trimming the margin of bouquets and baskets of flowers. The plant requires the highest hot-house temperature in winter, to develop the beautiful coloring of the leaves; under proper conditions it may be trained to a height or length of fifty feet.

Price 30 cents each; $3 per dozen.   The 3 sorts for 75 cents.

CYCLAMEN PERSICUM.

A fine ornamental greenhouse plant; its flowers, as a variety in the formation of bouquets and baskets of cut flowers in winter, are valuable; colors white, spotted crimson, &c.

Large plants $1 each; $9 per dozen; smaller, 60 cents each; $6 per dozen.

CHRISTMAS ROSE. (Helleborus Niger.)

A hardy herbaceous plant, which, in States south of Baltimore, is in full bloom at Christmas; flowers are single white, two inches in diameter, resembling a single rose-flower; at the north it is a valuable plant for cut flowers at Christmas or New Years.

Price 75 cents each ; $7 50 per dozen;

CLEMATIS.---(Virgin Bower.)

C. Amelia.
C. Azurea Grandiflora.
C. Flammula, white, fragrant.

C. Hybrida Splendens, large, fine form.
C. Louise, white.
C. Languinosa.

Price 50 cents each ; $4 50 per dozen. Set of six sorts for $2.

COLEUS, GOLDEN.

When, in 1869, the dark colored, or velvet-leaved Coleus were for the first time offered for sale in this country, they were gladly welcomed as desirable additions to a genus of plants that as yet comprised but a limited number of varieties; but in 1870, when the Golden section made their advent among us, their arrival was hailed with delight; as a plant for greenhouse decoration, they were unsurpassed, and the expectations that they would stand our sun well, have been fully realized. We have planted them out extensively the past four seasons, and they lost but little of their beautiful markings ; the test has fully established their permanency as a bedding plant for American gardens. Several of the most beautiful sorts we offer this season are home productions--superior to any we have had from Europe. For New Sorts see Novelties.

Golden Gem, deep crimson bronze, margined with bright sulphur yellow.
Albert Victor, centre purplish red, broad yellow margin.
Eclat, bronzy crimson, golden edge.
Favorite, fine crimson scarlet, golden edge.
Model, pinkish bronze, slight golden edge.
Nonesuch, deep shade of crimson, yellow edge.
Prince Leopold, cinnamon-red, deep yellow edge.
Princess Royal, centre reddish bronze, light yellow margin.
Red Cloud, brownish red, beautiful.
Setting Sun, rich bronze crimson centre, bright yellow edge.
Unique, reddish crimson, deep golden edge.
Chameleon, purple, rose and green, novel.
Bouquet, yellow, irregularly blotched with maroon.
Baron de Rothchilds, reddish brown, yellow margin.
Serena, rich cinnamon, yellow edge.
Juliet, light purplish red, broad yellow margin.
Edith, cinnamon, golden border.
Queen, brownish crimson, deep yellow edge.
Beauty of Widmore, white, green, maroon and pink. *Dwarf.*
Laciniata, canary, occasionally marked with cinnamon.
Mutabilis, reddish maroon, golden edge.
Princess of Prussia, purplish maroon, narrow yellow margin.

Price 25 cents each ; $2 25 per dozen. Set of 22 for $4.

COLEUS, VELVET (or dark colored.)

These are varieties, selected from upwards of fifty sorts in our collection, as giving the widest range of color, in the beautiful leaf-markings of this popular section.

Attraction, pea green, mottled with rich chocolate-colored spots.
Bauseii, deep chocolate crimson, leaves deeply serrated.
Excellent, deep shade of maroon, netted with light green.
Frou-Frou, changeable yellowish green, centre blotched with maroon.
Hamlet, purplish maroon.
Hero, chocolate maroon.
Hendersonii, purplish maroon, green margin.
Marshalii, rich chocolate purple, maroon green edge.
Refulgens, very dark maroon.
Rival, dark claret crimson, yellow edge.
Verschaffeltii, rich velvet crimson.
Veitchii, green margin, centre dark maroon.
Brunette, velvet maroon, splashed green.
Gigantea, rich purplish maroon, yellow edge.
Rainbow, leaves crinkled, purplish maroon, yellow edge.

Price 25 cents each ; $2 25 per dozen. Set of 15 sorts for $3. Full set of 37 sorts, Golden and Velvet, $6.

DRACÆNA. (Dragon Tree.)

Beautiful ornamental-leaved plants, much used for centres of baskets or stands.

Terminalis, rich crimson foliage. | Brasiliensis, broad deep-green leaves.
Indivisa, green and bronze, narrow leaves. | Ferrea, dark bronze leaves.

Draco, green, angular leaves.

Price 75 cents each, $7 50 per dozen ; 5 varieties $2.
Large size $1 50 each; 5 varieties $4 00.

DAHLIAS---New Seedling of 1873.

Raised by GERHARD SCHMITZ, Philadelphia.

Arabella, yellow shaded lilac. | Little Nymph, blush white, full centre.
Amethyst, lilac, large and fine. | Nero, crimson, full centre.
Adeline, pure white, tipped crimson, large | Rosette, rose edged lilac.
Augusta, yellow, tipped rosy lilac. | Symbol, yellow shaded rose.
Butterfly, yellow, tipped white. | Sensation, yellow tipped lilac.
Charmer, white, lilac centre. | Union, yellow edged lilac.
Ceres, rose shaded white. | Viola, rose shaded lilac.

Price 50 cents each. Set of 14 sorts, $5.

DAHLIAS---General Collection. (Large-flowering.)

In the selection of the varieties named we have discarded such sorts as do not come up to the requisite standard. The list as given below embraces, perhaps, the finest collection in this country, comprising every shade of color and marking. Strong plants ready in May ; dry roots of most sorts now ready. Many of the new and high-priced varieties of last season are included in this selection.

Ardens, yellowish pink.
Annie Boleyn, white, rose edge.
Admiral Stopford, scarlet and white.
Admiration, scarlet and blush.
Andrew Dodd, bright golden yellow.
Amazement, dark crimson.
Amazon, yellow, scarlet edge.
Angelina, yellow, striped and spotted carmine.
Autumn Glow, orange yellow.
Bizarre, striped.
Barmaid, white, salmon tipped.
Baron Alderson.
Belle dé Baum, deep pink.
Bismarck, crimson maroon.
Black Knight, very dark crimson.
Ball of Fire, scarlet.
Bob Ridley, dark scarlet.
Corsair, dark crimson.
Collossus, yellow.
Canary, fine yellow.
Copperhead, orange.
Charles Perry, dark maroon.
Coquette, violet striped and spotted carmine.
Crimson Monarch, fine crimson scarlet.
Criterion, bright rose.
Daisy, light scarlet.
Darkness, deep purple.
Disraeli, orange scarlet.
Duchess of Cambridge, blush, crimson tip
Duchess of Wellington, blush.
Dandy, striped carmine and white.
Dr. Boyes, dazzling scarlet.
Dr. Webb, deep scarlet.
Eliza Burgess, dark lilac.
Ellen, blush tipped lilac.
Emma Cheney, claret color.
Empress, white tinged violet.
Emily, white, fine.
Eva, blush white.
Flirt, striped yellow, scarlet and white.
Fancy Queen, crimson scarlet.

Flamingo, deep vermilion scarlet.
Fanny, light blush.
Flora, magenta shade.
Firefly, scarlet.
Fulgens Picta, scarlet, tipped white.
Golden Gem, clear yellow, perfect form.
Galathea, light rose, crimson striped.
Grace, blush.
Hendersoniana, deep scarlet.
Harlequin, salmon, tipped crimson.
Imperatrice Eugenie, crimson, tipped white.
John Bunn, yellow, striped crimson.
John Slade, dark maroon.
La Phare, dazzling scarlet.
Lilac Queen.
Mont Blanc, white.
Magician, crimson and white.
Martha, yellow, tipped scarlet.
Minette, maroon.
Miss Caroline, white, carmine edge.
Madame Zahler, scarlet and yellow.
Miss Trotter, blush, crimson edge.
Mrs. Burgess, bluish purple.
Mrs. Rollins, blush, tinged violet.
Mutual Friend, rosy salmon.
Neville Keene, light yellow, shaded lilac.
Norah Crena, orange, tipped rose.
Octoroon, lilac, crimson striped.
Oriole, golden yellow.
Picotee, lilac and white.
Pre-eminent, purple.
Picta, bright orange.
Roi de Pontales, purple, tipped white.
Rising Sun, bright scarlet.
Snow Storm, white.
Snowdrift, pure white, fine.
Sparkler, purple, tipped white.
Tom Green, maroon, tipped white.
Triomphe de Peck, deep crimson.
Vesta, pure white, very fine.
Wilson Hunt, scarlet crimson.

Price 30 cents each ; $3 per dozen. Set of 82 sorts for $15.

DAHLIAS, BOUQUET or POMPONE.

The great interest taken in this beautiful class has induced us to largely increase our variety, so that those which we offer this season include nearly every style and color embraced by the large-flowering sorts. The following include many of the finest new sorts of 1872 and '73. Strong plants in May; dry pot roots of most sorts ready now.

Advance, maroon.
Alba Floribunda Nana, white profuse.
Amorette, white tipped carmine.
Beatrice, blush, tinted violet.
Bessie, buff, shaded red.
Bicolor, scarlet, tipped white.
Black Dwarf, dark crimson.
Bride of Roses, light pink.
Child of Faith, white tinged blush.
Cochineal Rose, cochineal carmine.
Colonel Sherman, light scarlet.
Crimson Beauty.
Dr. Stein, dark maroon.
Flambeau, bright crimson.
Fairy Child, crimson.
Gem, crimson.
Goldlight, straw color and white.
Gros Von Tricken, crimson and scarlet.
Graphic, purple carmine.
Jennie, white, tipped violet.
Jewel of Austerlitz, fine scarlet.
Kind and True, straw color, purple tip.
K. Schawman, bright scarlet, fine form.

Little Beauty, crimson and white.
    "   Agnes, scarlet.
    "   Charles, amaranth and orange.
    "   Kate, dark crimson.
    "   Pet, amber, tinted violet.
    "   Rifleman, crimson and white.
L. T. Schminke, yellow, tipped scarlet.
Metropolitan Queen, large lilac.
Mary, pale rose.
Mein Strefling, salmon, striped crimson.
National, buff and crimson.
Otto Weilbacher, yellow, striped scarlet.
Penelope, blush, purple tip.
Perfection, deep maroon, fine form.
Pet of the Village, carmine crimson.
Princess of Lilliputs, blush, amber shaded
Prima Donna, rich crimson.
Rose of Gold, fine vermilion scarlet.
Sambo, dark maroon.
Sappho, rich crimson maroon.
Selmer, yellow, purple tipped.
Snowflake, pure white.
Seraph, buff, tipped orange.

Price 30 cents each ; $3 per dozen. Set of 46 sorts, $10.
Full assortment of 150 distinct sorts (large and small-flowered), for $30.

DAHLIA IMPERIALIS.

The flowers are single; the petals radiating from a yellow disc, are of the purest white, except a crimson spot at the base. The flower, which is bell-shaped and drooping, resembles a gigantic Lily, for when in full bloom the plant is from eight to ten feet in height, having from forty to fifty of these Lily-like flowers expanded at once. It blooms rather late for our latitude, unless the plants are very strong when planted out, but it is well worth a place in the conservatory. It does well in the Southern States.

Price 75 cents each; $7 50 per dozen.

DELPHINIUM BICOLOR GRANDIFLORUM.

This beautiful variety is increased by seeds, equally so as the well-known "D. Formosum," which it resembles in many respects, but with the improvement of having a much larger and clearer defined white centre, encircled by the richest shade of azure blue. It blooms almost without intermission from July to October, and, being entirely hardy, is a valuable acquisition to our herbaceous plants. See cut.

Large plants, 50 cents each; $4 50 per dozen. Smaller, 25 cents each; $2 25 per dozen; $15 per hundred.

DELPHINIUM MD. GERARD LEIGH.

A variety with azure-blue flowers, shaded with white; flower-spikes loose, six inches in length. This is a very distinct sort, and of a very rare shade of color.

Price 50 cents each; $4 50 per dozen. Smaller, 25 cents each; $2 25 per dozen.

DURANTA BAUMGARTII FOL. VAR.

A beautifully marked plant, resembling in the leaf-markings Sol. Pseudo Capsicum var., but of a taller and more branching habit. The leaves are marked to one-half their depth with golden yellow. An interesting plant at all seasons.
Price 30 cents each; $3 per dozen.

DIONEA MUSCIPULA. (Venus' Fly Trap.

A very interesting plant, a native of most of the Southern States. It takes its name of "Fly Trap" from a curious formation of the leaves, which are very sensitive. As soon as an insect touches them they close, and remain so as long as the insect continues to struggle. It is easily cultivated in a warm, moist atmosphere, such as a Wardian Case or Jardiniere.   Price 30 cents each; $3 per dozen.

DIANTHUS VERSCHAFFELTII.

Blooms in May and June, forming a most beautiful shaped plant; flowers white, ribbed with crimson, double, and two inches in diameter; fragrant.
Price 25 cents each; $2 25 per dozen.

DEUTZIA.

Small growing shrubs of great beauty. We offer two sorts of these, one pure white, and the other, not purple as its name indicates, but white, with the back of the petals tinged with purple or rose, varying as the flower fades.

| **D. crenata alba, fl. pl.** | **D. crenata purpurea, fl. pl.** |
| Small plants 30 cents each; $3 per dozen. | Large plants 50 cents each; $4 50 per dozen. |

ECHEVERIA SECUNDA GLAUCA.

ECHEVERIA.

A genus of succulent plants both novel and interesting. They are useful either as pot plants for decorative purposes, or for bedding out in summer. Being natives of arid countries they thrive best if planted in a dry situation, growing where most other plants would fail.

Echeveria Retusa Floribunda.	Echeveria Secunda.
" Metalica.	" " Glauca. See cut.
" " Glauca.	" Atropurpurea.
" Elegans.	" Splendens.

Price 30 cents each; $3 per dozen; $2 for set of eight.

ERYTHRINA CRISTA GALLI.---(CoralTree.)

A splendid genus of half-hardy shrubs, growing about five feet in height, with neat cut foliage, the stems terminated with spikes of rich scarlet, pea-shaped flowers. Grows freely if planted in a warm situation; should be treated the same as Dahlias.
Price 50 cents each; $4 50 per dozen.

EPIPHYLLUM TRUNCATUM. (Lobster-leaved Cactus.)

A very useful winter flowering plant; flowers in the different varieties, shading from purplish crimson, to scarlet. Six sorts.
Price for large plants, 75 cents each; 6 varieties, $3. Small, 30 cents each; 6 varieties, $1 50.

ERIANTHUS RAVENNÆ.

This ornamental grass when in full bloom attains a height of from nine to twelve feet, occasionally having over 50 flower spikes on one plant, in two or three seasons, from seed. It resembles the Pampas Grass, but blooms much more abundantly, and, with the advantage of being hardy, will prove a most desirable plant for the decoration of lawns. Seeds sown in our greenhouses last March produced plants which threw up flower-stems four feet in height by October. See cut.

Price 80 cents each ; $3 per dozen.

EUONYMUS RADICANS VARIEGATA.

A plant with small glossy pea-green leaves, deeply margined with creamy white ; well fitted for baskets.

Price 30 cents each ; $3 per dozen.

EUPHORBIA JACQUINIFLORA.

A well-known hot-house plant. flowering in mid-winter; from its wreathed style of flowering it is much used in holiday decorations; flowers orange scarlet.
Price 50 cents each ; $4 50 per dozen ; smaller, half price.

ERANTHEMUM ANDERSONII.

This charming plant is a native of India, and is not surpassed by any other plant in the beauty of its flowers, resembling some of the handsomest Orchids The spikes of flowers are borne on quite small plants. The two upper and lateral lobes are pure white, while the Orchid-like lip or lower segment is thickly dotted with crimson.

Price 50 cents each ; $4 50 per dozen.

ERANTHEMUM.

The species of this genus are very pretty ; some are cultivated for their foliage, and others for the beauty of their flowers, for which they are remarkable.

Igneum, dark velvety foliage, netted with bright yellow, flowers red.
Pulchellum, flowers blue, leaves splashed with silvery white.
Sanguinolentum, leaves veined with crimson, flowers red.
Price 50 cents each ; $4 50 per dozen. Set of 4 sorts, $1 50.

EUPATORIUM.

White winter flowering plants, the flowers of which are largely used in making up wreaths, crosses and baskets of cut flowers. They bloom very freely, doing best when planted out, becoming pot-bound soon.

Elegans, white, blooming from January to February.
Riparium, white, large truss, blooming from February to March.
Augustifolium, white, blooming from December to February.
Price 30 cents each ; $3 per dozen.

FEVERFEW. (Pyrethrum.)

P. Parthenium, flowers double, white; summer blooming.
P. Parthenifolium Aureum, "Golden Feather," golden yellow foliage.
Price 25 cents each ; $2 25 per dozen.

FERNS.

These beautiful plants are now very generally cultivated ; their great diversity and gracefulness of foliage make them much valued as plants for baskets, vases or rock-work, or as specimen plants for parlor or conservatory.
Price 30 cents each ; twelve beautiful sorts $3. Large plants 60 cents each ; $6 per doz.

FICUS REPENS.

A plant suited especially in greenhouse decoration, for covering the walls, pillars, &c., or for outside decorations in the South, as it clings to stone or wood work with the greatest tenacity, covering it with a mass of bright green foliage.
Price 30 cents each ; $3 per dozen.

FICUS REPENS MINIMA.

A miniature variety of the above.
Price 30 cents each ; $3 per dozen.

FUCHSIAS, Winter-flowering Sorts.

Carl Halt, corolla crimson, striped white.
Speciosa, corolla scarlet, two inches in length, sepals blush.
Gem, corolla violet, sepals crimson.
Puritana, corolla white, sepals dark crimson.
Aurora, corolla orange scarlet, sepals white, splendid.
Day Dream, corolla maroon, sepals crimson.
Price 30 cents each ; $3 per dozen. Set of 6 varieties for $1 50.

FUCHSIA ELM CITY.

FUCHSIAS---Best Early Flowering Market Sorts.

Wave of Life, foliage yellow, corolla violet, sepals crimson.
Brilliant, corolla bright scarlet, sepals white.
Prince Imperial, corolla purple, sepals recurved, crimson.
Elm City, double, buds forming large, globular, crimson scarlet balls. See cut.
Sinbad, corolla pure white, sepals rosy crimson.
Mrs. Marshal, corolla carmine, sepals white.
    Price 30 cents each; $3 per dozen. Set of 6 varieties for $1 50.

FUCHSIAS---General Collection.

Charming, corolla violet, sepals crimson.
Alba Coccinea, corolla dark purple, sepals white.
Annie Boleyn, corolla violet blue, sepals crimson.
Punch, corolla violet, sepals deep red.
Conspicua, corolla white, sepals violet crimson.
Diadem, corolla plum color, sepals vermilion.
Day Dream, corolla maroon, sepals crimson.
Pio Nono, corolla purple, sepals scarlet.
Symbol, corolla pure white, sepals rose.
Rose of Castile, corolla blush violet, sepals white.
Grand Cross, corolla double, dark violet, sepals crimson.

FUCHSIAS---General Collection---Continued.

Gov. Baker, corolla plum color, sepals crimson.
Sir Harry, corolla violet, sepals vermilion.
Tower of London, corolla double, violet blue, sepals crimson.
Albert Coen, corolla blush violet, sepals crimson.
Aucubæfolia, crimson corolla, sepals light.
Meteor, bronze leaves, very ornamental.
Bismarck, corolla double, maroon, sepals scarlet.
Souvenir de Cheswick, corolla violet, sepals red.
Empire, corolla pure white, sepals crimson.
Beauty of Sherwood, corolla cherry, sepals light.
Peeress, corolla violet, clear white sepals.
White Eagle, corolla white, sepals carmine.
Wonder, corolla violet, sepals vermilion.
Triumphans, corolla deep violet, sepals crimson.
Tribune, corolla double, violet, sepals scarlet.
Bird of Paradise, corolla rose, sepals crimson.
Mrs. Bennett, corolla white, sepals carmine.
Mrs. Lyndore, sepals vermilion, light purple corolla.
Violet Queen, corolla deep violet, sepals white.
Prince Napoleon, corolla purple, sepals waxy crimson.
Emperor of Brazil, corolla violet, flaked with rose, sepals scarlet crimson.
President MacMahon, corolla scarlet, sepals greenish yellow.
Amphion, very dwarf and early, corolla plum color, sepals crimson.
General Werder, corolla light rose, sepals crimson scarlet.
Inimitable, early variety, an improvement on Prince Imperial.
Mrs. Thorley, corolla pure white, sepals rich crimson, recurved.
Lady Heytesbury, corolla violet, sepals pure white.
Warrior, corolla plum color, sepals scarlet crimson.
Striata Perfecta, corolla carmine, striped white, sepals pure white.
Bright Heart, corolla pure white, sepals pinkish crimson.
Dolly Varden, double corolla, violet, sepals scarlet.
Little Harry, light purple, sepals waxy crimson.
Miss Arthur, corolla orange scarlet, petals blush.
Herculaneum, double corolla, deep violet, sepals vermilion.
Dreadnaught, double purplish corolla, sepals carmine.

Price 30 cents each; $3 per dozen.   Full set of 58 sorts, $12.

GAZANIAS.

Low growing plants, with large showy flowers varying through all the shades of orange and yellow, blooming all summer. Are excellent for baskets or rock work.
Price 30 cents each; $3 per dozen.

GENISTA CANARIENSIS.

A broom-like plant, with spikes of bright yellow flowers. The plant grows into a nicely shaped shrub of from 2 to 4 feet in height, suitable for parlor or greenhouse culture; is hardy in Southern States.
Price 30 cents each; $3 per dozen.

GLOXINIA.

Hothouse plants, blooming during the summer months; flowers violet, white, scarlet or crimson, borne upright, or drooping in the different classes.
Price 30 cents each; $3 per dozen.

GESNERIA.

Plants of the same natural order as the Gloxinias, many of them having rich velvet-like foliage.   Price 30 cents each; $3 per dozen.

GERANIUMS, SCENTED.

Apple, 50c.	President Thiers, 50c.	Quercifolium Nigricans.
Atrolinæfolium,	Lady Plymouth.	Pennyroyal.
Blandfordianum.	London Blue, 50c.	Rose.
Citron.	Little Pet, ex.	Rose, variegated, 50c.
Dr. Livingston.	Filicifolia, 75c.	Skeleton leaved.
Lemon.	Querc folium.	Shrubland Pet.

Price 30 cents each; except where noted. Set of 18 sorts $4 50.

GERANIUM, VARIEGATED ROSE-SCENTED.---True.

A variegated variety of the Rose Geranium; fragrance the same as in the parent variety; leaves fringed with creamy white, sometimes assuming a pinkish tinge, which gives a unique and interesting appearance to the plant.
Price 50 cents each; $4 50 per dozen.

GERANIUMS ZONALE.

This class of plants having proved so admirably adapted for bedding purposes in our hot and dry summers, are now cultivated in larger quantities than any other plant, with the exception, perhaps, of the Verbena. A bed of Geraniums, consisting of nearly a hundred varieties, was one of the finest sights in our grounds last season. Below will be found a list comprising old standard varieties, and embracing many of the newer and finer sorts of our late importations. The cut above is a fair representation of this class, in its various colors.

Antagonist, dark orange scarlet.
Aurora, cherry pink, nosegay.
Beaton's Perfection, bright pink, nosegay.
Belle Helene, salmon pink.
Blue Bells, fine mauve (*not blue.*)
Bridal Beauty, white, banded rose color.
Chance, large, bright scarlet.
Magenta Christina, rose pink.
Colensii, crimson scarlet.
Duchess of Sutherland, carmine pink.
Dr. Lindley, rich orange scarlet.
Echo, large, rosy crimson.
Elegans, deep rosy salmon.
Father Ignatius, extra large, scarlet.
Fire King, rich dazzling scarlet, black zone.
Gen. Montelambert, dark scarlet, ornamental foliage.
Gen. Scott, salmon rose.
Gloire de Corbonay, salmon pink, 50c.
Hector, light dazzling scarlet.
Helen Lindsay, deep carmine pink.
Incomparable, striped, 50c.
Indian Yellow, light orange scarlet.
Dr. Newham, large cherry white eye.

Beaton's Rival, crimson.
King of Pinks, deep pink.
Gen. Grant, fine large scarlet.
Jean Sisley, finest scarlet, 50c.
Improvement, dark pink.
Laviata, orange scarlet.
Marie L'Abbe, white, rosy pink centre.
Md. Rendatler, pink.
Master Christine, rich pink, 50c.
Minnie, crimson, nosegay.
Mons. Barre, rosy pink.
Mrs. Whitty, pink, nosegay.
Minnahaha, rose and white.
Ossian, crimson scarlet.
Prince of Wales, salmon, tipped white.
Regulator, large, light scarlet.
Sheen Rival, rosy scarlet.
Successful, orange scarlet.
Theresa, white, carmine eye.
Union, light scarlet, white eye.
Wonder, carmine crimson, ornamental foliage.
Winter, orange scarlet.
Waltham, bright scarlet.

Price 30 cents each ; $3 per dozen, except where noted. Set of 46 sorts, $10.

GERANIUMS, LILLIPUTIAN ZONALE.

Amelia Grissau, salmon, margined white.
Aurantia striatia, bright salmon.
Beauty of Surrey, pink.

Bridesmaid, salmon rose.
Bicolor, deep salmon eye, 50c. each.
Clipper, large light scarlet.

GERANIUMS, LILLIPUTIAN ZONALE---Continued.

Cybester, orange crimson, nosegay.
Dr. Koch, dark scarlet.
Rustic Beauty, intense scarlet, bright eye
Chas. Reust, salmon, shade white.
Little Dorrit, beautiful salmon pink.
Md. Wherle, white, pink eye.
Md. Rudersdoff, salmon and white.
Queen of the Dauphin, light scarlet, very large.
Roi d'Italia, large scarlet, white eye.
Emily Vauchier, white, red anthers.
Francis Dubois, white salmon centre.

International, crimson.
Jules Favre, crimson, white eye.
Little Gem, bright scarlet, white eye.
Leonadis, large, light scarlet.
Little Harry, bright crimson scarlet.
Little Dear, light pink.
Rival, orange scarlet.
Snowflake, pure white.
Symmetry, violet crimson.
Troubadour, carmine.
Village Maid, rose color.

Price 30 cents each ; $3 per dozen. Set of 28 sorts, $6. Complete set of 74 sorts, both classes, for $15.

GERANIUM ZONALE, BICOLOR.

This is one of the best of a comparatively new type. As we try to represent in the engraving, the ground color of the flowers is nearly pure white, the centre marking being of a rich, deep salmon shade of rose. This style of Geranium will yet be new to many of our customers, and we therefore again give illustration. The leaves are lightish green, with a clearly marked dark zone. See cut. Price 50 cents each ; $4 50 per dozen.

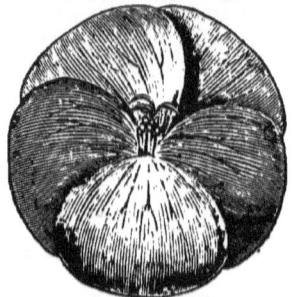

ZONALE GERANIUM, "Jean Sisley."

Not quite a new variety, but one of the finest in cultivation. It is of dwarf habit, forming large trusses of flowers of the most *brilliant scarlet*, having a distinct white eye or centre. We have over 100 varieties of the finest Zonale Geraniums in our collection, but consider this variety unequaled. See cut.

Price 50 cents each; $4 50 per dozen.

ZONALE GERANIUM, "Master Christine."

A fitting companion for the variety "Jean Sisley" before described, similar in all respects except that the ground color is *deep rose* with a white centre.

Price 50 cents each; $4 50 per dozen.

GERANIUMS, DOUBLE.

We have increased our already large assortment of this superb class, by the addition of several new and distinct varieties.

Andrew Henderson, dark scarlet.	Francois Defour, carmine.
Ascendency, light rose.	Md. Lemoine, bright rosy pink.
Delight, dark rose.	Marie Lemoine, dwarf pink.
Emily Lemoine, deep pink.	Md. de St. Paul, pale vermilion.
Jeanne de St. Maur, bright vermilion.	Princess Teck, largest and best scarlet.
Glorie de Nancy, deep carmine.	Triomphe, rich shade of scarlet.
La Vesuve, large scarlet.	Triomphe de Lorraine, bright carmine.
Latonia, fine formed scarlet.	Victor Lemoine, the earliest and most
Marie Crousse, lightest shade of pink.	profuse blooming scarlet.
Floribunda, large and fine, rich dark red.	Wilhelm Pfitzer, dwarf, flowers scarlet.
Aline Sisley, see special description, 50c.	Basilisk, deep pink.
Admiration, see special description, 50c.	Charles Darwin, deep carmine.
Asa Gray, see special description, 50c.	Madame Abel, rich shade of rose.
Le Negre, see special description, 50c.	Refulgent, ruby crimson.
La Promise, see special description, 50c.	Charles Lyell, salmon pink, distinct.
Emilio Castelar, crimson, extra.	Hero of Strasburg, salmon, shaded crimson
Brigantine, scarlet.	Brilliant, blood red.
Victor of Lyons, light violet.	Comet, violet crimson.

La Vengeur, dark crimson.

Price 30 cents each, except where noted; $3 per dozen. Full set of 36 sorts, $7 50.

GERANIUMS---PELARGONIUMS---General Collection.

The following sorts we select from our collection of over fifty varieties, as possessing the greatest contrast in color, besides being the finest growing and most prolific flowering sorts. We do not attempt to describe them, as the colors are so blended in this beautiful class, that any description that can be given conveys but little idea of what the variety is like.

Auguste Odier.	Captivation.	Madella D'Or.	Mazeppa.
Belle Blonde.	Crimson King.	Eclipse.	Scaramouch.
Bride.	Naomi.	Lady Mary Fox.	Virginia.
Lady Blanche.	Morganii.	Larina.	Majestic.
Comte de Paris.	Touchstone.	Cardinal Richelieu.	Advance.
Britannia.	Reine Hortense.	Comet.	Cambria.

Price 50 cents each; $4 50 per dozen. Set of 24 sorts, $7 50.

GERANIUMS---PELARGONIUMS.---12 Best Market Sorts.

Gen. Taylor.	Md. Pescatore.	Mazinella.
Dr. Andry.	Agnes.	E. G. Henderson.
Belle de Paris.	Alba Multiflora.	Sir Jas. Asher.
Beadsman.	Rodriques.	Washington.

Price 50 cents each; $4 50 per dozen.

GERANIUM, Mrs. POLLOCK.---Golden Tricolor.

The ground color of the leaf is deep green : next comes a zone of bronze crimson, the margin of which is tinted with scarlet ; then again a belt of lighter green, the margin of the leaf being clear yellow. As an ornament for the parlor or conservatory, nothing yet excels this beautiful *class*, of which **Mrs. Pollock** is a type ; the flowers are dark scarlet, in good sized trusses, borne on short foot stalks but a few inches above the leaves. It succeeds well in the open border in early summer and in fall, but during the hot months of July and August loses, to some extent, the rich coloring of the leaves. The leaves are much used in bouquets in winter.

Price 50 cents each ; $4 50 per dozen.

GERANIUMS, GOLD, SILVER, AND BRONZE LEAVED.

The varieties as named below are selected from nearly fifty sorts in our collection, as being the best representatives of this deservedly popular class of plants. Although in our hot and dry summers the beautiful markings of the leaves are, to a certain extent, lost, yet, as a plant for greenhouse or parlor culture, nothing is more worthy of cultivation. They are now, perhaps, the most popular plants we cultivate as house plants, and their leaves being extensively used in baskets and bouquets of cut flowers in winter, large portions of the space in our greenhouses are occupied by them.

Arthur Wells, bronze-leaved, flowers scarlet.
Alma, leaves dark green, silver margined.
Beauty of Oulton, light green maroon.
Black Hawk, dark bronze zone on a yellow ground.

GERANIUMS, GOLD, SILVER AND BRONZED LEAVED, Continued.

Perilla, chocolate zone, yellow edge.
Stella, leaves green, dark zone, white edge.
Queen of May, white, green, bronze and pink.
Bijou, flowers dazzling scarlet, leaves silver margined.
Bronze Queen, leaves yellowish brown, with dark zone, flowers crimson.
Bronze Model, light brown, dark disc.
Beauty of Caulderdale, one of the best bronze.
Cherub, deep green and white, flowers carmine.
Battersea Park Gem, golden and green, flowers scarlet.
Cloth of Gold, golden yellow, with dark green marking.
Flower of Spring, leaves straw color, flowers scarlet.
Fontainbleau, green, zoned black, margin sulphur white.
Glowworm, sulphur white, with bronze zone.
Golden Pheasant, golden yellow, crimson, black and yellow.
Golden Fleece, greenish yellow leaves.
Golden Vase, golden-margined, cherry-colored flowers.
Honeycomb, green disc, rosy violet.
Jane, disc of leaf bright green, pure white margin.
Lady Cullum, improvement in "Mrs. Pollock."
Little Pet, white, pink and green, variegated.
Mrs. Pollock. (*See special description.*)
Mountain of Snow, pure white margined, scarlet flowers.
Neatness, yellow ground, chocolate margin.
Silver Pheasant, leaves white, carmine and green.
Silver Queen, light green, margined white, flowers rose.
Sunset, color golden yellow, veined with crimson.
Italia Unita, zone carmine, flowers scarlet.
Quadricolor, brown, pink and white.

Price 30 cents each ; $3 per dozen. Set of 32 sorts, $7 50.
For other sorts, see "New and Scarce Plants."

GERANIUM, MOUNTAIN OF SNOW.

We have experimented with a large number of varieties of variegated Geraniums, with a view to developing those having the best qualities for bedding purposes. This kind we find to possess a growth as vigorous as the common scarlet varieties, retaining its variegation of foliage during our hottest and driest weather. As a bedding plant for its foliage, it is admirably suited. It is also like all other variegated Geraniums, beautiful as a pot plant.

Price 30 cents each ; $3 per dozen.

GERANIUMS, IVY-LEAVED.

Although the foliage of this class is of sufficient interest to warrant its cultivation, yet the value is greatly enhanced by the beauty and profusion of its flowers during the spring and summer months, running through the various shades of white, pink and crimson. The list below is selected as giving the widest range of color. They are well adapted for rock work or vases, and for drooping over baskets,.or trained on trellises, are unsurpassed; few plants give more satisfaction for house culture. One-half of those named below are the high-priced sorts of previous years.

Bridal Wreath, flowers pure white.
Butterfly, white, spotted rose.
Diadem, deep carmine.
Elegans, rose and white.
Elegans Variegatum, varieg'd foliage, 50c.
Fairy Bells, violet and white.
Floribunda, deep pink profuse.
Gem, flowers white and purple.
Coccinea, scarlet flowers, 50c.
Lady Edith, carmine rose, fine.

Holly Wreath, leaves blotched white.
Innocence, pure white, in large trusses.
L'Elegante, variegated, 50c. (*See cut.*)
National, rich carmine, veined white.
Princess Alexandria, pink.
Princess Thyra, white and pink.
Remarkable, rose and white, upright habit.
Speciosus, white ground, violet spotted.
Wilsii, neat erect habit, magenta.

Price 30 cents each, except where noted; $3 per dozen. Full set of 19 sorts, $4 50.

GLADIOLUS, FRENCH HYBRID.

The varieties of this beautiful class are now so numerous, and many of them so much resembling each other, that we do not give a descriptive list of varieties. Our collection however, is very select, embracing about thirty distinct sorts. Gladiolus, by planting every two weeks (from 1st May to 1st July,) will give a succession of bloom from July until November. The bulbs are of the easiest culture, never failing to bloom. Our prices this season, owing to the large stock we hold, are much reduced. They are now so low that beds exclusively of Gladiolus may be planted at small cost. Our seedling bulbs are of large size, embracing hundreds of varieties, and at prices lower than we have ever before offered them.

Price 25 cents each; $2 50 per dozen. 50 choice flowering bulbs, in 25 named sorts, $7 50. 100 choice flowering bulbs, in 25 named sorts, $12.

The same unnamed, 10 cents each; $1 per dozen; $8 00 per 100.

GNAPHALIUM TOMENTOSUM.
GNAPHALIUM LANATUM.

White- leaved plants, suitable for narrow ribbon-lines or baskets. **G. Tomentosum** has narrow lanceolate leaves two inches in length; grows to a circumference of twelve inches. **G. Lanatum** is of more vigorous growth.

Price 30 cents each; $3 per dozen. The 2 sorts, 50 cents.

HOYA CARNOSA.

Or Wax Plant; has thick fleshy leaves, growing moderately fast, and bearing um-
bels of beautiful flesh-colored flowers, from which are exuded large drops of honey-like
liquid. One of the best plants for house culture, as it stands the extremes of heat and
cold better than most plants, and is not easily injured by neglect. It can be trained to
climb on trellis work to almost any height, and when in bloom—which continues for
upwards of three months—is a most interesting plant.

Price 30 cents each ; $3 per dozen.

HELIOTROPES.

Caroline des Antoines, lilac blue.
Cardinal Richelieu, lavender blue.
Duc du Lavendury, rich blush, dark eye.
Garibaldi, almost white.
Le Geant, very light, large.
Reptans Major, lavender and white.
Migniome, lilac.
Beauty of Bordeaux, lavender.
Incomparable, light, very fragrant.

Florence Nightingale, light lavender.
Beauty of Oulton, lilac blue.
Gen. Vanhambert, light lavender.
Madam Facilon, bluish violet.
Little Negress, very dark blue.
Md. Michel, bluish violet, light centre.
Mrs. Burgess, dark violet.
Maculata, purple, white spot.
Star, 50 cents.

Price 25 cents each ; $2 25 per dozen. Set of 18 sorts, including "Star," $3.

HELIOTROPE, "Star."

One of the darkest varieties, of neat dwarf growth, having an immense truss of very dark violet or purple flowers, deliciously fragrant.

Price 50 cents each ; $4 50 per dozen.

HYDRANGEA HORTENSIS.

An old hardy shrub of great merit, growing about two feet in height, the stems being terminated with large heads of pinkish flowers, changing to bluish purple. Hardy with slight protection.

Price 30 cents each ; $3 per dozen.

HOLLYHOCKS.

Too well known to need any description, combining in their flowers a large variety of color, from pure white to crimson, and perfectly double. 12 distinct sorts.

Price 50 cents each ; $4 50 per dozen.

HIBISCUS. (Chinese.)

Hibiscus Rosa Sinensis, single red.
" Rosa Sinensis Aurantiaca fl. pl., double orange.
" Rosa Sinensis Cooperii, foilage variegated, white, green and pink.

Price 50 cents each : $4 50 per dozen.

HABROTHAMNUS ELEGANS.

Strong growing plants, bearing panicles of carmine flowers. Their beauty and free flowering properties entitle them to a place in every collection. They do well when forced for winter flowers.

Price 30 cents each ; $3 00 per dozen.

IVIES, ENGLISH, (Hedera).

Hedera Elegantissima.
" Rhombia.
" Maculata.

Hedera Chrysacarpa.
" Donrailensis.
" Helix, (common English.)

Price 30 cents each ; $3 per dozen. Set of 6 sorts, $1 50.

IVY, GERMAN OR PARLOR. (Senecio Mikanoides.)

A rapid growing, climbing plant with yellow flowers, well adapted for covering trellis work quickly, or as a house plant in winter—leaves glossy green.

Price 25 cents each ; $2 25 per dozen.

IPOMŒA MORTONII.

A new and valuable climber or creeper, well suited either for climbing on trellis work, or drooping over the sides of baskets or vases—flowers pinkish lilac ; it grew upwards of 20 feet high during July and August of last summer with us.

Price 30 cents each , $3 per dozen.

IPOMŒA MACROHIZA.

A climber, which from its rapid growth, is well suited to cover trellises or any other objects where a quick growing vine is wanted. It is very vigorous, perennial, tuberous rooted, with white flowers borne in August.

Price 30 cents each ; $3 per dozen.

JASMINUM GRANDIFLORUM.---Catalonian Jessamine.

A valuable winter-flowering plant, either for parlor or greenhouse, blooming without intermission from October to May. The flowers are pure white, most deliciously fragrant ; used extensively by all bouquet makers.

Price 30 cents each ; $3 per dozen.

JASMINUM REVOLUTUM.

A yellow flowered Jasmine, growing rapidly to about the height of ten feet. A splendid plant for the Southern States, as it is hardy south of Maryland. Very fragrant.

Price 30 cents each ; $3 per dozen.

JESSAMINE (CAPE)---Gardenia Florida, Radicans, and R. Variegata.

Strong plants, 50 cents each ; $4 50 per dozen ; 3 sorts $1. Smaller plants, 30 cents each ; $3 per dozen. 3 sorts, 75 cents.

JUSTICIA COOPERI.

A neat variegated leaved plant, with bright carmine flowers. Blooms during the spring and winter months

Price 50 cents each ; $4 50 per dozen.

KONIGA MARITIMA VARIEGATA.---(Var. Sweet Alyssum.)

This is one of our most useful variegated plants, the white of the foliage predominates over the green, making the plant in the summer season one of the very best we have for massing, or in ribbon-lines, in contrast with dark foliage. It is also excellent for baskets, and as it blooms freely in winter, its sweet scented white flowers are much used for bouquets. See cut.

Price 25 cents each ; $2 25 per dozen.

LAMIUM MACULATUM, ALBUM AND RUBRUM.

Old, hardy, herbaceous plants, but now rather scarce ; the leaves are dark green, marked down the centre with a broad well-defined white stripe. The flowers, which are formed in short round spikes, are of the purest white in one sort, and red in the other.

Price 25 cents each ; $2 25 per dozen.

LASIANDRA MACRANTHA.

A very free growing plant, introduced from Brazil, giving, when two or three feet high, a profusion of fine saucer shaped flowers, of a rich violet blue color.

Price 50 cents each ; $4 50 per dozen.

LINUM FLAVUM.

A plant of the flax order, of extremely neat habit, growing about one foot in height, with flowers of pure yellow, nearly two inches in diameter, almost covering the plant when in full bloom.

Price 30 cents each ; $3 per dozen.

LANTANAS.---General Collection.

We have few continuous blooming plants that afford a greater variety of color than the Lantana. It is yearly becoming more extensively cultivated, so that it ranks as one of the most important plants that we grow. The varieties named below have been selected from our importations of the last few years, as the most distinct.

Adolph Avas, canary, dark centre.
Alba, white.
Alba Perfecta, pure white, very fine.
Aurantiaca, bright orange.
Clotilda, pink, centre yellow.
Delicatissima, deep lilac.
Don Calmut, orange.
Eugenie, rose and white.
Flora, orange and pink.
Fulgens, yellow and orange.
Flava Lilacina, lilac and orange.
Flaviana, canary.
Grand Sultan, purple and yellow.
Hendersonii, rose, centre white.
Lina Etinger, straw color, dwarf and profuse.

Lenain, orange and carmine.
Magnum, large white, yellow centre.
Marcella, lilac rose, changing to yellow.
Md. Porcher, rose and salmon shaded.
Mons. Bucharlet, golden yellow, changing to yellow.
Monfeck, crimson, compact habit.
Mutabilis Major, orange and scarlet.
Md. Caillotte, orange red, yellow centre.
Md. Hoste, rose and orange.
Raphael, purple, orange and rose.
Rubra Lutea, red and yellow.
Splendens, purplish red.
Triumph, dark orange.
Victoria, white, lemon centre.
Wm. Schull, rose and yellow.

Price 25 cents each ; $2 25 per dozen. Set of 30 sorts, $5.

LINARIA CYMBALARIA VARIEGATA.---(Kenilworth Ivy.)

A very interesting variegated variety of the ordinary Toadflax, of a dense and dwarf growth, never exceeding four inches in height, and of a creeping or trailing habit. The leaves are finely marked to one-half their depth with sulphur-white. Invaluable for rock-work, and very desirable for baskets or vases. Scarce. See cut.
Price 30 cents each ; $3 per dozen.

LILY OF THE VALLEY.---(Convallaria Majalis.)

This beautiful little plant is extensively grown for forcing in the winter and early spring months, the pendulous grace of its white flower-spike being much prized in the construction of the most valuable baskets and bouquets. It is entirely hardy, preferring a position slightly shaded.
Price 25 cents each ; $2 25 per dozen ; $15 per hundred.

LAVENDULA CRISTATA.

A species of Lavender, with finely gray colored leaves, delicately scented.
Price 30 cents each ; $3 per dozen.

LILIUMS.---In Variety.

Seldom, on the introduction of a class of plants, has so much interest been taken as in the case of the Japan Lily. So popular have they become that where we annually sold hundreds a few years ago, we now sell thousands. Those named below embrace all the leading Japan sorts, together with a few of the finest of the other varieties. The Liliums are entirely hardy, and with but few exceptions are of the most delicate fragrance ; the coloring of some of the Japan varieties—crimson on white or rose grounds—is beautiful in the extreme. Our stock this season of the Japan sorts is large and fine, and in many sorts still further reduced in prices.

Lilium Auratum, fine bulbs	$0 75 each ;	$7 50 per dozen.	
" Candidum, pure white	30 "	3 00 "	
" Fortunii, a variety growing from 6 to 7 ft. in height	50 "	4 50 "	
" Lancifolium Rubrum, (red spotted)	30 "	3 00 "	
" " Roseum, (rose spotted)	30 "	3 00 "	
" Longiflorum, trumpet shaped, white	30 "	3 00 "	
" Tigrinum Splendidum,	50 "	4 50 "	
" Bulbiferum,	30 "	3 00 "	
" Thunbergianum,	30 "	3 00 "	
" Umbellatum, deep red	50 "	4 50 "	
" Maculatum, dark red, yellow spotted	50 "	4 50 "	
" Aurantiacum, orange	30 "	3 00 "	
" Umbelliferum, flowers borne in umbells	30 "	3 00 "	

LONICERA.---(Honeysuckle.)

Brachypoda, valuable for its remarkably vigorous growth, flowers yellow, fragrant.
Flexuosa, an old favorite, holding its leaves during nearly the entire winter; flowers variegated, red, yellow and white, sweet scented.
Halliana, another evergreen Honeysuckle, with very fragrant white flowers.
Belgicum, blooms throughout the season, flowers fragrant, red and yellow.

First size, 50 cents each ; $4 50 per doz.   Second size, 25 cents each ; $2 25 per doz.

LIBONIA FLORIBUNDA.

A neat growing greenhouse shrub, attaining a height and breadth of twelve or fifteen inches. The flowers, which are about an inch in length, are scarlet orange at the base, running into deep yellow at the top, in some degree resembling a Manettia. It blooms in the greatest profusion from December to May, and is a great acquisition to our winter blooming plants.

Price 30 cents each ; $3 per dozen.

BEDDING OR DROOPING GREENHOUSE LOBELIAS.

Among the most useful plants for hanging baskets, or for the front or outside row in ribbon lines. Their dwarf habit, and the profusion of their charming little blue and white flowers, render them exceedingly ornamental.

Emperor William, large deep blue.	New Double, 75c. new. See colored plate.
Erecta Compacta, light blue.	Compacta, violet.
Globosa, rounded bush, dark blue.	Queen Victoria, rich blue, white eye.
Miss Murphy, white, compact habit.	Cinderella, light.
Paxtonii, blue, white eye.	Purple Prince, purplish lilac.
Brilliant, dark rich blue.	Ivory Pearl, pearly white.

Price 25 cents each, except where noted.   Set of 12, including the New Double, $8.

LYCHNIS FLOS CUCULI PLENO.---(Double White Lychnis.)

A valuable plant for summer bouquets ; flowers pure white, two inches in diameter, resembling a double Carnation. It blooms from middle of June to October ; entirely hardy in this section.

Price 30 cents each ; $3 per dozen.

LYSIMACHIA NUMMULARIA.---(Moneywort.)

This old and well known plant is indispensable for drooping around the edges of baskets or vases, its graceful stems often falling four feet from the edges of a basket or vase It is attractive at all times, but particularly so in June, when covered with its rich yellow flowers.

Price 25 cents each ; $2 25 per dozen.

LYSIMACHIA NUMMULARIA AUREA.

A variety of the above, with bright yellow foliage, which will prove, from its drooping habit, to be very valuable for our basket plants.

Price 30 cents each ; $3 per dozen.

MIMULUS.---In Variety.

Strikingly handsome flowers, among the gayest ornaments of the greenhouse or flower garden.

Moschatus, (Musk Plant) yellow.

Tigrinus, an exceedingly beautiful new blotched and spotted hybrid, rivaling the Calceolaria in the variety of its brilliant color.

Price 30 cents each ; $3 per dozen.

• MANETTIA.

Neat graceful summer blooming climbing plants, having flowers in great profusion the entire season ; excellent for training on any kind of trellis work.

Bicolor, flowers scarlet, tipped yellow.

Cordifolia, crimson scarlet.

Price 30 cents each ; $3 per dozen.

RED CRAPE MYRTLE. (Lagerstræmia Elegans.)

A well known shrub ; one of the most beautiful, common to the Southern States where it is hardy. When grown North, it should be kept in pots or tubs, and kept in a dry cellar in winter.

Price 50 cents each : $4 50 per dozen.

WHITE CRAPE MYRTLE. (Lagerstræmia Indica Alba.)

A white flowering variety of this beautiful shrub we believe, has been comparatively unknown until lately. A plant in bloom was shown during the month of September at one of the greatest Horticultural Exhibitions ever held in Louisville, and was the wonder and admiration of thousands. The treatment of the White Crape Myrtle is in all respects the same as required for the Red Crape Myrtle.

Price 75 cents each ; $7 50 per dozen   The two sorts for $1.

MADEIRA, or MIGNONETTE VINE.

One of the best plants for rapidly covering trellis work. Flowers feathery white, with fragrance of Mignonette.

Price 15 cents each ; $1 50 per dozen.

MAHERNIA ODORATA.

A neat growing greenhouse plant, blooming in the early spring months ; flowers yellow, bell shaped, of exquisite fragrance.

Price 30 cents each : $3 per dozen.

MYOSOTIS, IMPERATRICE ELIZABETH.---(Forget-me-not.)

A lovely variety of the well-known Forget-me-not. blooming profusely during the
spring months, and continuing to flower, though sparingly, throughout the summer;
form of growth is dense and dwarf. Flowers beautiful lilac blue shade, with yellow centre.
Price 30 cents each; $3 per dozen.

MYOSOTIS DISSITIFLORA.---(Forget-me-not.)

This pretty little plant, when in bloom, is about 9 inches high literally covered with
its rich blue flowers, each floret having a round white spot in its centre.
Price 30 cents each; $3 per dozen.

MYRSIPHYLLUM ASPARAGOIDES.---(Smilax.)

There is no climbing plant in cultivation that surpasses this in the graceful beauty
of its foliage, and its peculiar wavy formation renders it one of the most valuable of all
plants for vases or hanging baskets, as it can be used either to climb or to droop, as required; in cut flowers, particularly for wreaths, it is now considered indispensable by all
florists. Its hard texture enables it to keep without wilting for several days after being
cut. Its cultivation has now become a specialty in every large city, greenhouses being
devoted solely to its cultivation. For a parlor or window plant it is indispensable. See
cut.
Price 25 cents each; $2.25 per dozen; $15 per hundred.

MESEMBRYANTHEMUM.---"Wax Pink."

Aurantiacum, dark orange.
Cordifolium, pink.
  " Variegatum, 50 cents.
  See novelties.

Blandum, white.
Deltoidum, pink.
Nitidum, white.
Aureum, yellow.

Price 30 cents each, except where noted ; $3 per dozen. Seven sorts for $2.

NERIUM.---(Oleander.)

Macrophyllum, deep carmine.
Nivium, pure white.
Variegatum, white and red.

Shaw's Seedling, crimson.
Carneum, large double pink.
Lutescens, straw color.

Price 50 cents each ; $4 50 per dozen. Set of six sorts for $2 25.

NIEREMBERGIA RIVULARIS.

A perennial herbaceous plant, a decided acquisition to our basket and bedding plants. The plant is of a creeping habit, rising only a few inches from the ground ; flowers pure white, with yellow disc; flowering from June to September. A splendid plant for cemeteries, or where other hardy white flowers are desired. See cut.

Price 30 cents each : $3 per dozen.

NIEREMBERGIA GRACILIS.

A well known bedding plant, of slender grass-like habit, with bluish white flowers, an inch in diameter, flowering from June to October.

Price 30 cents each; $3 per dozen.

ORNITHOGALUM UMBELLATUM.---(Star of Bethlehem.)

An interesting bulbous rooted plant, blooming in June, with narrow green leaves. striped white. The flowers are pure white, star shaped, and exceedingly pretty. They have the peculiarity of opening at eleven in the morning, and closing at three in the afternoon.

Price 30 cents each : $3 per dozen.

PANSIES.---General Collection.

Our stock of Pansies has been much improved by saving only from the best flowers, so that now a large proportion of our own seedlings are equal to European varieties. For New White Pansy, see novelties.

Price 15 cents each ; $1 50 per dozen ; $9 per hundred. Finest French Fancy, extra choice, 30 cents each ; $3 per dozen ; $18 per hundred.

PANICUM VARIEGATUM.

A variegated grass of drooping or creeping habit, a valuable plant for baskets or vases. Its style of growth is peculiarly graceful ; the color of the leaves is dark green, white and rose, the white and green being about equally divided, the rose shade margining the white slightly. It attains a diameter of two feet in a few months' growth, and thus developed is exceedingly beautiful. It grows best in partial shade.

Price 30 cents each ; $3 per dozen.

PASSIFLORA.---(Passion Flower.)

These beautiful and interesting plants climb to a height of 20 or 30 feet if desired— "P. Cærulea"—the variety shown by cut, is hardy with slight protection in this latitude —colors varying in the different sorts, blue, crimson, white, etc.

Passiflora Pfordti.   Passiflora Trifasciata.
   "   Cærulea. See cut.   "   Alata.
   "   Van Volxemi.

Price 30 cents each ; $1 for five varieties

PENTSTEMONS.

This beautiful class make fine plants of from eighteen inches to two feet in height, and are in continuous bloom from the time they are planted out until frost; flowers in spikes of Gloxinia-like form, shaded and mottled in all colors of white, blue, scarlet, crimson and pink.

Decasaine, sulphur, pink tinted.
Euclide, crimson, feathered purple.
Mc. Christine, carmine, white throat.
Livingston, carmine, white throat.
Souvenir de M. Cernet.
Mrs. Theney, crimson, violet throat.
Md. Christine.

Robert Heggett.
Mons. Parette, purplish black, blush tube.
Pauline Dumont, crimson, white throat.
Princess Alice, blush purple and white.
Rubra Magnifica, red and white.
Sir Harry, pink and red.
Tom Pouce, blush, shaded crimson.

Price 30 cents each ; set of fourteen sorts for $3.

POINSETTIA PULCHERRIMA.

A tropical plant of gorgeous beauty, the bracts or leaves that surround the flower being, in well grown specimens, one foot in diameter, of the most dazzling scarlet. In a hot-house temperature of 60 degrees, it begins to bloom in November, and remains expanded until February. This peculiarity of blooming in the heart of Winter makes it largely in demand for baskets and vases of cut flowers at the holidays in our large cities. During the holiday week of last year we sold 3000 heads of Poinsettia, at an average of 16 cents each.

Price 25 cents, 50 cents, $1 and $3 each, according to size.

DWARF POMEGRANATE.---(Punica Nana.)

A dwarf variety of Pomegranate. It has the peculiarity of flowering profusely, while not more than a foot in height. Well grown specimens grow about six feet in height, by three feet in diameter; plants of this size in bloom are truly magnificent. The color of the flower is a peculiar shade of orange scarlet, a very rare color, brilliant in the extreme. The plant blooms from October to December. As it is deciduous, after blooming, it can be kept in a cellar or under the stage of a greenhouse, until it is time to start it to grow again in May. In any of the States where the thermometer does not fall to fifteen degrees below freezing, it is entirely hardy. See cut.

Price 50 cents each ; $4 50 per dozen.

POMEGRANATE.---In Variety.

Punica Granatum. red.   Punica Granatum Album, white.
Punica Granatum Album Plenum, double white.

Price 50 cents each ; $4 50 per dozen. Four sorts for $1 50.

PILEA SERPÆFOLIA AND REPTANS. (Artillery Plant.)

Unique plants, with graceful frond-like leaves, which when in flower, produce a snapping sound when water is thrown on the leaves.

Price 25 cents each ; $2 25 per dozen.

PETUNIAS, SINGLE.

The engraving will give some idea of the handsome markings of the single Petunias. We have hundreds of varieties, from seed, varying through all the shades of crimson, carmine and rose to purest white, striped, mottled, and self-colored.

Price 15 cents each ; $1 50 per dozen.

PETUNIAS.—Double.

Wm. White, crimson and white.
Magnet, white and maroon.
Snowball, pure white.
Rosalind, violet.
Goliah, large crimson lilac.
Mrs. Bliss, white, crimson stripes.
Royal Purple, very double, fine form.

Mad. de la Vergne, large blush, pink veined.
Eva, purple and white.
Miss S. Frost, crimson, rose and white.
Marmorata, pink, spotted, white.
Queen of Whites, fine shaped, white.
Sable Queen, purplish maroon.
Rudolph, white striped lilac.

Price 30 cents each ; $3 per dozen ; set of 14 sorts, $3.

PLUMBAGO.

Two rather scarce greenhouse shrubs, producing large trusses of blue flowers during the fall and winter months. Plants six inches in height, flower freely, and as the color of their flowers is rare, they are indispensable additions to any collection.

Capensis, light blue. | Larpentæ, dark blue.

Price 30 cents each ; $3 per dozen.

PAMPAS GRASS.---(Gynerium Argenteum.)

A stately species of grass from South America, growing six feet in height, with plumes of yellowish white, one to two feet in length ; it looks best as a single specimen. As it is not quite hardy North, it requires protection of eight or ten inches of leaves around the roots, or it can be removed to the cellar, and replanted in spring.

Price 50 cents each ; $4 50 per dozen.

PERISTROPHA ANGUSTIFOLIA VARIEGATA.

A beautiful variegated plant no longer new, but which has as yet had but a limited distribution ; as a plant for hanging baskets, or for ribbon lines in massing, it is particularly valuable ; it forms a compact bush 6 inches in height and about 1 foot in diameter ; the leaves are beautifully marked with golden yellow and green, the yellow predominating.

Price 30 cents each : $3 00 per dozen.

PHLOX, HARDY HERBACEOUS.—General Collection.

As this beautiful genus of plants bloom well in partial shade, they are, perhaps, the most valuable plants we cultivate for city gardens or shrubberies. Our collection embraces every color from purest white to darkest crimson. They are entirely hardy in all sections of the country. They bloom in immense trusses, and are, therefore, well adapted for exhibition. The new sorts of 1873 are included in this collection.

Albertus, shaded purple and crimson.
Auriel Duriez, pure white, carmine eye.
Boree, violet crimson.
Coquette, pink and white.
Dominican, crimson rose.
Don Carlos, rose.
Drusus, crimson rose.
Eliza Brozner, white, rosy eye.
Etoile du Neuilly, white, pink centre.
Gem, blush, purple eye.
Hendersonii, crimson purple, scarlet edge.
Louis Weinrich, rosy lilac.
Madame Bellvenue, rose, crimson centre.
" Corbay, white, violet centre.
" Cubitier, white, crimson edge.
" de Wendall, white, vermilion eye.
" Duchemin, white, shaded red.
Liervali, dark rose, striped with white.
L'Avenir, fiery red, immense truss.
Mad. Froment, pure white, purple centre.
William Bull, lilac, white centre, extra large.
Souvenir de Berryer, crimson, purple centre.
Madam Moisette, violet ground, scarlet centre.
Mons. Guldenschuck, rose, purplish scarlet centre.

Flora M'Nab, delicate pink, crimson centre.
Madame Pepin, beautiful lilac pink.
" Rendatler, blush, crimson eye.
" Van Houtte, pure white, crimson eye.
Mdlle. Ladonette, blush, large crimson eye.
Mr. Roberts, pink, purple shaded.
President Morell, blush, cherry eye.
Princesse de Bonheur, white, violet eye.
Raphael, violet, white centre.
Roi des Roses, rosy salmon, scarlet eye.
Semiramis.
Victor Hugo, large deep purple.
" Lemoine, cream, purple centre.
White Lady, purest white, 50c.
Lothair, light scarlet, shaded with violet.
Miss McCrae, pure white, dark purple centre.
Mrs. Laing, rosy lilac, perfect form.
Princess Louise, snow white, carmine centre.
Chancy, rich dark rose color, fine form.
Czarina, pure white, very dwarf and compact.
Citoyen de Caprera, white, shaded with violet. [rose.
York and Lancaster, striped white and

Price 30 cents each ; $3 per dozen ; full sets of 40 sorts, $10.

PHLOX, HARDY HERBACEOUS.---White Lady.

A pure white variety, rarely exceeding eighteen inches in height, with flower-trusses six inches in diameter ; one of the most beautiful of all white flowering, hardy plants.   Price 50 cents each ; $4 50 per dozen.

FORCING PINK, "Lady Blanche."

A rose-petalled, *pure white* variety, double, of fine form and clove fragrance ; it is equally prolific in bloom as the well-known, white-fringed pink, but having much larger and finer formed flowers.   Price 60 cents each.

FORCING PINK, " Coccinea."

Color scarlet, entirely different from any other pink, being more like a Carnation except in its dwarf habit, which is only about 1 foot when in full flower.   We brought the stock of this variety from London in fall of 1872, but had not stock enough of it to offer until last season.   It is of the richest clove fragrance.
Price 60 cents each ; the 2 sorts for $1.

PINK, ALBA FIMBRIATA.

A double white sort, of good form and substance ; quite fragrant, and extensively grown around New York, for forcing during the winter months.   Like the rest of its class, it is excellent for summer bouquets. Flowers double, fringed, one inch in diameter ; entirely hardy.
Price 25 cents each ; $2 25 per dozen ; $15 per hundred.

PINKS, FLORISTS'.

These are dwarfer than the Carnation, growing about one foot in height, the colors being of the various shades of maroon, carmine and rose, beautifully laced with white flowers perfectly double, clove-scented ; *plant entirely hardy.*   The following varieties embrace all shades and styles ; indispensable for summer bouquets.

Annotdale.	Defiance.	Lady Blanche, 60c.	Pumila.
Alice.	Earl of Carlisle.	Mrs. Hobbs.	Queen Victoria, 60c.
Alfred Harrington.	Esther.	Mrs. Stephens.	Rose of Sharon.
Brunette.	Emil.	Mrs. Pottifer, 60c.	Rose of England.
Claude.	General Lafayette.	Nina.	Tennyson.
Coccinia, 60c.	Juliet.	Optima.	Tom Long.
Coopers' Attraction, 60c.	Kohinoor, 60c.	Plato.	Variabilis.
	Laura Wilmore.	Prince Arthur.	

25 cents each, except where noted ; $2 25 per dozen ; set of 30 sorts, $6 00.

MULE PINKS.

Pinks of dwarf, neat growth, about 9 inches in height, flowering continually during the summer ; flowers rosy carmine.
30 cents each ; $3 00 per dozen.

PINKS, HYBRID JAPAN.

Comprising over a dozen distinct and beautiful varieties ; colors white, crimson, rose, violet, maroon, &c., &c.; double and fragrant ; exceedingly well adapted for summer bouquets ; blooms from June to November.
Price 15 cents each ; $1 50 per dozen.

PRIMROSE, DOUBLE WHITE CHINESE.

Perhaps this is the most profitable of all plants we cultivate for winter flowers, well-grown specimens, from November to April, yielding often 500 flowers. Our stock is large, and plants in fine health ; always a scarce plant, being slow of increase.
Large plants, $1 50 each ; $12 per dozen ; smaller, $1 each ; $9 per dozen.

PRIMROSE, CHINESE, SINGLE RED AND WHITE.

One of our first winter blooming plants, the single varieties blooming more profusely than the double sorts, and of easier culture ; they make splendid plants for the parlor in winter.
Large plants, $1 each ; $9 per dozen ; smaller, 50 cents each · $4 50 per dozen.

PEPEROMIA MACULOSA.

A very useful plant for baskets, the neat character of the foliage rendering it very ornamental, resembling in habit the **Rex Begonia.**
Price 30 cents each ; $3 per dozen.

RHYNCOSPERMUM JASMINOIDES.

A beautiful climber, not unlike a Jasmine, with pure white flowers, deliciously fragrant ; valuable for forcing in winter, the flowers of which are much in demand by bouquet makers.

Price 50 cents each ; $4 50 per dozen.

RHYNCOSPERMUM JASMINOIDES VAR.

A variety of the above, with foliage very prettily variegated with green, white and carmine.

Price 50 cents each ; $4 50 per dozen.

REINECKEA CARNEA.

A dwarf-growing, grass-like plant, bearing purple flowers ; an excellent plant for aquariums, the margins of fountains, &c.

Price 30 cents each ; $3 00 per dozen.

RUELLIA FORMOSA.

A winter-flowering, salvia-like plant, bearing flowers of the most brilliant scarlet during the entire winter months.

Price 30 cents each ; $3 per dozen.

ROSES.

It will be seen that this year we have changed the general arrangement of Roses, placing them more in regard to their hardiness and blooming qualities, than botanically. The Monthly or Ever-Blooming sorts, undoubtedly give better satisfaction than the Hybrid Perpetuals – flowering continually—but not being hardy north of Maryland require protection (which is best done by covering the roots in December with leaves or coarse litter to about six inches in depth.) The Hybrid Perpetuals are perfectly hardy, but do not bloom, as their name would indicate, perpetually, giving only one profuse bloom in June, and a partial bloom throughout the summer.

All, with but few exceptions, are grown on their own roots, from cuttings of the young wood ; they are healthy plants, that have never been forced, and are grown in pots. We would here take occasion to state the great advantage to the buyer to get Roses that have been *grown in pots.* The fact of their having been so grown in no way affects their hardness, but on the contrary, enables them to grow with vigor from the time they are planted, while those lifted from the open ground take half the summer before they commence to root, many of them dying outright. We never sell Roses from the open ground unless specially ordered, and never do so without warning the purchaser of the risk of failure.

Purchasers will always do better to leave the selection of varieties to us, as far as possible, not only as a rule getting better plants, but, besides, greater distinction of varieties.

ROSES, MONTHLY OR EVER-BLOOMING.

TEA.

Adam, large, pinkish purple.
Belle Alamande, blush.
Bella, pure white, see special description.
Bon Silene, see special description.
Belle Macconaise, salmon rose.
Bianquii, french white.
Camellia, pure white.
Cels, blush, profuse bloomer.
Compte de la Carthe, deep blush, ex.
Catharine Mermet, blush.
Duchess de Brabant, see special description.
Duc de Cayes, yellowish white.
Isabella Sprunt, see special description.
Leveson Gower, rosy salmon.
Marie de Bau, rich blush.
Melville, pink.
Madame Bravy, globular white.
Md. Trifle, salmon yellow.

Madame Maurin, pure white.
" Ristori, blush.
" Russell, light pink.
" de Vatry, carmine rose.
Md. Hippolyte Jamain, yellow and white
Md. Azalie Imbert, orange yellow.
Marie Van Houtte, yellowish white.
Nina, large pinkish rose.
Odorata, blush.
Olympe Fraguip, sulphur yellow.
Pauline Lebonte, light blush.
Premiere de Charissimes, violet pink.
President, light salmon.
Souvenir de Elise Vardon, creamy white
Safrano, see special description.
Stella, light yellow.
Souvenir d'un Ami, light lilac.
White Tea.
Yellow Tea, straw color.

Buyer's selection, 60 cents each ; $6 per dozen. Our own selection, 50 cents each ; $4 50 per dozen. Full set of thirty-seven varieties of Tea Roses for $12. For new Tea and those figured in colored plate, see novelties.

WINTER FLOWERING TEA ROSES.

Safrano, orange yellow.   Isabella Sprunt, canary yellow.

The two leading winter-flowering Roses; probably twenty thousand plants of these varieties are grown, planted out and in pots, to produce "Tea" Rose Buds in winter for the New York bouquet makers. We ourselves use 10,000 square feet of glass for this special purpose.

Bon Silene.

An old sort, but now attracting attention as a variety valuable for forcing for Winter flowers. It has long been extensively grown around Boston, but its value has only begun to be realized in other parts of the country lately. It is a true Tea Rose, having the delicious odor of that class; the color is peculiarly bright, but of a shade difficult to describe—a blending of purple and carmine, with the slightest shade of orange.

Bella.

This Rose has now proved a standard sort. We have propagated it largely, and now offer it as low as other Roses. It is entirely free from mildew, and is exceedingly valuable for what is so much wanted—white rosebuds during the summer and winter months.

Duchess de Brabant.

One of our most valuable summer and winter blooming varieties, equally good for either season, free bloomer, color light carmine, tinged violet, buds full and very fragrant. It ranks among the best of our winter flowering Roses.

Prices of the above *Winter Blooming Roses*, first size, 50 cents each; $4 50 per dozen; second size, 25 cents each; $3 25 per dozen. Set of five sorts, large size, $2; second size, $1.

BOURBON AND BENGAL.

Agrippina, bright crimson.
Appoline, cupped carmine.
Beau Carmine, light crimson.
Bosanquet, blush white.
Bourbon Queen, rich blush.
Bouquet de Marie, deep pink.
Cramoise Superior, purplish crimson.
Compte Bobinsky, rich crimson.
Compte d'Ue, purplish crimson.
Duchess Thuringe, French white.

Louis Phillipe, crimson.
Geo. Peabody, crimson.
Hermosa, pink, extra.
Laurencii or Fairy Queen, crimson.
Malmaison, deep blush.
Pierre St. Cyr, rosy carmine.
Paxton, large carmine.
Rio de Cramoise, red.
Sombriel, French white.

Buyer's selection, 60 cents each; $6 per dozen: our own selection, 50 cents each; $4 50 per dozen; full set of nineteen sorts for $6.

ROSES, BEDDING.

These are nice healthy plants, grown in smaller pots than the above, and we can therefore sell them at much lower rates. Last year these same sized plants gave such general satisfaction, that this season we have grown them much more extensively. Most of the varieties of Roses named in the preceding list of Teas, Bourbon and Bengals, are included in this selection. The kinds, however, must be of our own selection.

Price 20 cents each; $2 per dozen: $15 per hundred.

☞ Our selection of sorts only, but all named varieties.

NOISETTE OR CLIMBING MONTHLY.

Triomphe de Rennes, canary color.
Caroline Manais, blush white, extra.
Climbing Devoniensis, pale yellow.
Lamarque, large pure white.
James Sprunt, (see special description.)
Reve D'Or, (climbing safrano,) buff.

Marshal Neil, (see special description.)
Madame Longchamps, pure white.
Rosamond, scarlet crimson.
Setina, dark crimson.
Washington (White,) flowers white.
Gloire d'Dijon, salmon yellow.

Extra size, fine plants, $1 each; $9 for set of twelve.

NOISETTE, OR CLIMBING MONTHLY ROSE "James Sprunt."

This will prove a valuable acquisition as a pillar rose for greenhouses at the North, and for out-door culture South, as it will no doubt prove entirely hardy in most situations south of Baltimore. It grows to the height of six to ten feet in one season, blooming monthly. The bud is of rich dark crimson, getting somewhat lighter when expanded. Tea fragrance. It is probably a "sport" from the well-known monthly crimson Rose Agrippina; but its quick, vigorous growth makes it valuable as a climber. It was raised by Mr. James Sprunt, of Keenansville, N. C., the same gentleman to whom we are indebted for the far-famed yellow Tea Rose, "Isabella Sprunt."

Large stock plants, $1 each; second size, 50 cents each; $4 50 per dozen; third size, 25 cents each; $2 25 per dozen.

ROSE, MARSHAL NEIL.

This is now established as a standard sort; the bud is of the largest size, of a deep canary yellow; it partakes more of the Noisette than the Tea class, in our opinion, being a strong and vigorous grower, equal to **Solfataire** or **Lamarque**. Nothing exceeds the beauty of this Rose when planted out in the greenhouse, and trained to the rafters, or in the Southern States, where it is entirely hardy, on the piazza or on trellises. The *buds* sell to the bouquet makers here from 25 to 50 cents each in winter.

Price $1 each; $9 per dozen; second size, 50 cents each; $4 50 per dozen; third size, 25 cents each; $2 25 per dozen.

HARDY ROSES, Remontant or Hybrid Perpetual.

Achille Gonad, deep blush.
Augusta Mie, deep blush.
Adonis de Lyons, rosy blush.
Baron Provost, rich pink.
Cardinal Patrizzi, brilliant crimson.
Chas. Leferve, reddish crimson.
Compte de Paris, rich blush.
Cymabie, violet crimson.
Duplessis Morney, carmine crimson.
Eugene Sue, light crimson rose.
Geant des Battailes, scarlet crimson.
General Forney, clear red.
General Jacquimenot, crimson scarlet.
General Lane, dark rose.
General Washington, scarlet crimson.
Gloire of Waltham, crimson purple.
Imperatrice Josephine, blush.
Jules Margottin, bright deep crimson.
La Reine, satin rose,
Louis Verger, carmine crimson.
Louis Carriege, carmine.

Md. Knorr, pink.
Madame C. de Islay, light rosy blush.
    " Laffay, light crimson, very fragrant.
    " de Willermots, cup-shaped, ex.
Mrs. Chas. Wood, brilliant red, changing to rose.
Mrs. Reynolds, cupped carmine.
Peerless, (see special description.)
Pæonia, reddish crimson, ex. fine.
Pius IX, crimson violet.
Princess de Rohan, violet crimson.
    " Matilda, deep blush.
Purple of Orleans, purplish violet.
Reine d'Angleterre, fine bright rose.
Reine des Violets, dark violet.
Sydonia, light blush.
Triomphe de Alencon, bright crimson.
    " de Exposition, crimson red.
    " de Reims, light rose.
William Penn, light crimson, or pink.

Buyer's selection of sorts, 60c. each ; $6 per dozen ; our selection, 50c. each ; $4.50 per dozen ; set of forty sorts for $15. 100 varieties of Roses, Tea, Bourbon, Bengal (Monthly,) and Hybrid Perpetual for $30.

Peerless.

This was shown by our colored plate of 1872. To those having that plate, no description will be necessary, as it is a perfect representation ; to those who have not, we will say that it is entirely hardy ; flowers in immense clusters of rich crimson ; double, of fine form, and very fragrant.

Price for large plants, $1 50 each ; for smaller plants, 75 cents each ; $6 per dozen.

ROSES, HARDY GARDEN.

Md. Plantier.

A perfectly hardy pure white double Rose, of the Hybrid China class. One of the best white Roses there is ; it is excellently adapted for cemetery decoration, etc.; growth free and vigorous.

Price 60 cents each ; $6 per dozen.

CLIMBING.—HARDY.

Baltimore Belle, blush white.
Boursalt Elegans, purple crimson. (tion.
Gem of the Prairies. (See special descrip-

Seven Sisters, blush and crimson.
Prairie Queen, purple, veined white.
Scarlet Greville, crimson scarlet.

Extra large plants, in pots, $1 each ; $9 per dozen ; per set of six, $4 50.

Gem of the Prairies.

Is a hybrid between the well-known climbing rose, Queen of the Prairies, and the hybrid perpetual, Madame Laffay ; it possesses the climbing qualities of the prairie Rose, with the richness of color and delicious fragrance of the Hybrid Perpetual. The color is of a light shade of crimson, occasionally blotched with white. The flowers are large, perfectly double, and of fine form, which are borne on trusses, numbering from ten to twenty buds on each. This has now become a standard sort, possessing, as it does, all the habits of a climber, with the color of the hybrid perpetual class.

Price for large plants, $1 each ; $9 per dozen ; second size, 50c. each ; $4.50 per dozen ; strong young plants 25c. each ; $2 25 per dozen.

MOSS.—Imported.

White Bath, white.
Laneii, crimson.
Selina, dark crimson,

Adelaide, carmine.
English or Scotch, true, deep pink.
Marie de Bois.

Large plants, $1.50 each ; six varieties for $6 ; smaller, 75c. each ; six varieties for $3.

RICHARDIA ALBA MACULATA.

A plant belonging to the same order as the Calla Ethiopica, with beautifully spotted leaves. It flowers abundantly during the summer months, planted out in the open border. The flowers are shaped like those of the Calla, and are pure white, shaded with violet inside. It is a deciduous plant, kept dry in winter, and started in spring like a Dahlia.
Price 50 cents each; $4 50 per dozen.

STEVIA.

White winter blooming plants, of great value, in style of growth and free flowering qualities resembling the "Eupatorium," (although botanically distinct) and requiring the same treatment.

Compacta, compact, truss of snowy white, blooming earlier than, and continuing in bloom longer than any other variety; is best from November to January.
Serrata, a free flowering variety, blooming best around the holidays.
Price 30 cents each; $3 per dozen.

SCUTTELARIA.

Scarce and beautiful plants, the ends of the branches of which are terminated with spikes of brilliantly colored flowers; very ornamental.

Mocciniana, scarlet and yellow. | Purpurea, rosy purple.
Pulchella, rosy crimson.
Price 30 cents each; $3 per dozen.

SALVIA.

Rosea, see novelties. Rose colored, 50c.
Splendens, (scarlet Sage) flower spikes of the most brilliant scarlet.
 "   **Gordonii.** This differs from the above variety in being much more dwarf, flowering throughout the summer and winter.
 "   **Alba**, a white var. of "Splendens," identical in every respect, except in color, which is pure white; it is rather dwarfer than the scarlet, and contrasts well when planted in lines in front of it.
Patens, a variety well suited to contrast with the scarlet, the flowers being of the richest shade of blue.
Fulgens var., a winter flowering sort, with bright scarlet flowers, the foliage variegated with creamy white.
Officinalis var., a beautiful tri-colored variety of the common Sage; leaves white, green and pink blotched.
Price 30 cents each; $3 per dozen. Set of seven sorts, $1 50.

SANCHEZIA NOBILIS.

A hot-house plant, with broad, lance-shaped leaves, beautifully veined and marbled with orange yellow. Comparatively new and scarce.
Price 30 cents each; $3 per dozen.

SELAGINELLA (LYCOPODIUM)---Mosses.

Plants used in wardian cases or ferneries, and in some styles of cut flower decorations; require partial shade and a moist atmosphere.
Price 30 cents each; $3 for set of twelve.

SEMPERVIVUM.---House Leek:

A succulent genus of plants allied to the Sedums. The plants assume symmetrical table-like forms, many of them very novel and interesting. Both Sempervivums and Sedums are well adapted for culture in parlors or sitting-rooms, as they grow freely in a dry atmosphere, and can hardly be injured in any way except by an over-supply of water.
Price 30 cents each; $3 per dozen. Set of nine sorts for $2.

SEDUM.---Stone Crop.

We have to offer this season forty distinct species of Sedums, all of them interesting and many of them very beautiful, both in foliage and in flower.
Price 30 cents each; $3 per dozen; full set of thirty species, $6.

SOLANUM, IN VARIETY.

Capsicastrum, (*Jerusalem Cherry*.) A variety bearing bright scarlet berries in the fall and winter months, making it very ornamental.
Pseudo Cap Var. A variegated variety of the above.
Jasminoides Of more slender growth, adapting it for hanging baskets, etc., leaves variegated with white and green; the edges having a purple tint.
Price 30 cents each; $3 per dozen.

SAXIFRAGA SARMENTOSA.

A low growing plant, much like a Strawberry in habit, with leaves marked with silvery white. Excellent for hanging baskets or rock work.
Price 25 cents each; $2 25 per dozen.

TRITOMA GRANDIFLORA.

A very beautiful herbaceous plant, that ought to be in every garden. The flower-stalk grows to the height of three feet; the flower-spike is about one foot in length, of colors varying from yellow to deep scarlet, giving it somewhat the appearance of a heated bar of iron, hence it is vulgarly called "Red Hot Poker Plant." It continues in bloom from July to October, and grown either singly or in masses, produces a striking effect.   Price 30 cents each; $3 per dozen.

TALINUM PATENS VAR. (Basella Rubra Variegata.)

A beautiful species of half shrubby style of growth, the leaves are succulent, variegated green and white. It stands the hot dry Summer to perfection, and is a very great addition to our basket or vase plants. The flowers are pinkish carmine.
Price 30 cents each: $3 per dozen.

TRADESCANTIA.

Vulgaris (*Wandering Jew*.) A drooping sort, with bright glossy green leaves.
Zebrina. Leaves striped with silvery white on a dark ground.
Crassula. A strong growing variety, with white flowers.
Aquatica. See novelties. 30c.
Rupens Vittata. See novelties. 30c.
Price 25 cents each, except where noted; $2 25 per dozen. Set of five sorts, $1.

THYME.

Three ornamental varieties of the common Thyme, well suited for baskets, or margins of flower beds. They are all as equally useful for culinary purposes as the common sort.
Price 25 cents each; $2 25 per dozen; set of three sorts, 75 cents.

TORENIA ASIATICA.

One of the prettiest Summer plants for vases or hanging baskets; flowers blue, of a Gloxina-like shape, flowering during the summer months.
Price 30 cents each; $3 per dozen.

TRICYRTIS GRANDIFLORA.

A beautiful herbaceous plant, blooming during October and November.
Price 50 cents each; $4 50 per dozen.

TIGRIDIA. (Shell Flower.)

One of our favorite Summer-flowering bulbs, of the easiest culture, displaying their gorgeous tulip-like flowers of orange and scarlet daily from July to October.

Conchiflora, yellow. | Pavonia, red.
Price 25 cents each; $2 25 per dozen.

TROPÆOLUMS.

Excellent plants for the flower border in Summer, blooming in profusion from June till November. Extensively used for rock-work and vases. They bloom best in poor rocky or sandy soil.
Price 25 cents; $2 25 per dozen; $1 50 for set of eight.

TUBEROSES DOUBLE.—All Flowering Roots.

1st quality, started in pots for early flowering, $3 per dozen; 2d do., $2 per dozen.
1st quality, dry roots, $1 50 per doz.; $9 per hundred. 2d do., $1 per doz.; $7 50 per hundred. 3d do., 75c. per dozen; $6 per hundred. *New Tuberose "Pearl."—see Novelties.*

VIOLETS, SWEET SCENTED.

The varieties named below are the leading ones used here for for forcing during the Winter months. We need hardly state that the Violet now forms one of the principal items in the formation of Winter flowers.

Double White. | Marie Louise, dark blue flowers, larger
Double Blue Neapolitan, light blue. | than the "Neapolitan."
Shonbrun, flowers purple, single. |
30 cents each; $3 00 per dozen. Price for set of four sorts, $1.
Extra large plants of these sorts in the Fall, at double the above rates.

VINCA.—(Periwinkle.)

Vinca Major Variegata. | Vinca Argentea Variegata.
" " Cærulea. | " Elegans.
Price 30 cents each; $3 per dozen; four sorts for $1.

VERONICAS.

A beautiful class of plants, blooming during the fall months. The flowers are borne on spikes from four to six inches in length, and are produced in great abundance, running through the various shades of purple, rose, lilac and white.

Gloire de Lorraine, blue and white. | Creme et Violet, 60c. See novelties.
Imperialis, 60c. See novelties. | Mammoth, purple and white.
Variegata, foliage margined white. | Marmorata, rose color.
Blue Gem, dwarf habit, mauve. | Triomphe de Meaux, deep lilac.
Price 30 cents each, except where noted; $3 per dozen. Set of eight varieties, $2 50.

VERBENAS.—General Collection.

As is well known, the cultivation of the Verbena has for many years been our leading specialty. The present collection is the best sixty varieties we can select from the many hundred kinds we have in cultivation. Besides comprising old standard sorts, the present list embraces many of the newer and higher-priced sorts of 1874. Our plants are always strong and healthy, and are grown in small pots, well fitted for transportation. For new sorts, see page 10.

Argus, rosy pink, white eye. | Blue Bird, large deep blue.
Ajax, rich crimson, yellow eye. | Bismarck, blood red, white eye.
Aurora, striped salmon and pink. | Cærulea, large fine blue.
Ball of Fire, dazzling scarlet. | Conchiflora, shell-like pink.
Black Hawk, dark maroon. | Crimson Glow, deep crimson, violet eye.
Beauty of Sherwood, the best scarlet. | Distinction, ruby red.

VERBENAS.—General Collection.—Continued.

Echoline, light vermilion, yellow eye.
Formosa, large pink, white eye.
Gleam, large crimson scarlet, yellow eye.
Sable Queen, crimson, floret one inch in diameter.
Iona, large scarlet, yellow eye.
Ivanhoe, rich blue, white eye.
Imperatrice, striped lilac and white.
London Pride, large, claret-colored.
Mattie, pure white, rose margin.
Mary, large crimson, white eye.
Rosy Morn, deep carmine.
Austerlitz, blood red, white eye.
Anaceron, dark crimson, yellow eye.
Belle Davis, bright scarlet, white eye.
Cornet, bright ruby crimson, yellow eye.
Cyclop, rich blue.
Eyebright, rosy crimson.
Giant, rich scarlet, yellow eye.
Gen'l Dix, rich maroon, white centre.
Ida, large rose, white eye.
Jewell, bright scarlet.
Rover, maroon.
Peri, scarlet.
Miniola, rich crimson, yellow spot.
Macbeth, carmine, violet eye.

Miss Annie Massey, violet, shading to white.
Mary Baker, creamy pink.
Purple Queen, rich purple, white centre.
Pre-eminent, large rosy salmon, white eye.
Punctata, spotted and striped carmine.
Red Cap, blood red, white eye.
Ruby Queen, ruby, violet eye.
Sylph, pure white.
Senator, magenta, white eye.
Splendor, bright scarlet.
Sparkler, dark scarlet.
Virginale, large, pure white.
William Dean, violet blue, white eye.
William Young, large deep scarlet.
Zenobia, purple, large white eye.
Marmorata, striped.
Monstrosa, dark purple.
Notable, white, splashed with purple.
Surprise, large rosy pink, yellow eye, extra.
Social, mixed violet and crimson.
Viola, deep violet, fine form.
White Beauty, white.
Don Juan, white, bordered pink.
Mrs. Wilson, striped.

Price 15 cents each : $1 50 per dozen ; collection of 60 sorts, $6.

Those sorts in Heavy Type, were represented by our colored plate of last year, and are particularly fine.   Price 20 cents each ; $2 per dozen.

Full collection of 90 named sorts, new and general collection $10; *Scarlet, Blue, White,* or other kinds, in separate colors, $7 50 per hundred ; mixed unnamed Verbenas, 12 best distinct colors, $1 per dozen, $6 per hundred.

VALLOTA PURPUREA.

An old but rare autumn flowering bulb, growing from 12 to 15 inches in height, bearing flowers of purplish carmine, exceedingly beautiful.   Price $1 each.

SELECT HARDY HERBACEOUS PLANTS.

We offer a large collection of hardy herbaceous plants, among which are a number that are scarce and valuable.   They are all grown in pots, and can be transplanted, with certainty to live, at any time
Price 30 cents each ; $3 per dozen.   Set of 100 varieties, $18.

ORNAMENTAL LEAVED GRASSES.—Hardy.

Admirably adapted for massing in flower beds, and some of them are among the most graceful plants that can be used for hanging baskets or vases.

Acorus Variegatus, leaves glossy green and white.
Aira Cærulea Var., of erect and graceful habit; flower stalks well above the foliage.
Erianthus Ravennæ, (See cut, p. 30.)
Panicum Plicatum fol. var., attains a height of 4½ feet, leaves streaked carmine.
Isolepsis Gracilis, light green, wiry leaves, for baskets.
Gynerium Argentium, (*Pampas Grass.*) 50 cents.
Phalaris Arundinacea picta, var. ribbon grass.
Bambusa Japonica, low growing, for aquariums, etc.
Price 30 cents each ; $3 per dozen, except when noted.   Set of eight, $2.

PLANTS IN SPECIAL SELECTIONS.

Many of our customers being unable to determine what plants are best suited for a continuous display of flowers and foliage during the summer months, we submit the following, which we are satisfied will prove satisfactory, being our own selection, and of such plants as we grow in large quantities.   A saving of 30 per cent. is made in ordering from these selections.

SELECTION No. 1.—$25. *Numbering 200 Plants.*

12 Monthly Roses.	6 Chrysanthemums.	2 Pinks.
6 H. Perpetual Roses.	6 Scented Geraniums.	12 Gladiolus.
36 Verbenas.	2 Lemon Verbenas.	2 Abutilons.
6 Heliotropes.	6 Scarlet Salvias.	8 Begonias.
6 Fuchsias.	2 Blue "	6 Violets.
6 Zonale Geraniums.	2 Double Feverfew.	4 Double Geraniums.
4 Gold & silver-edged do	6 " Tuberoses.	
4 Ivy-leaved do	12 Petunias.	
6 Dahlias.	6 Ageratum.	
6 Lantanas.	6 Centaureas.	
6 Coleus & Achyranthes	6 Bouvardias.	
6 Lobelias.	4 Monthly Carnations.	

PLANTS IN SPECIAL SELECTIONS.—Continued.

SELECTION No. 2.—$15. *Numbering 100 Plants.*

8 Monthly Roses.	3 Variegated Geraniums	4 Double Tuberoses.	4 Coleus & Achyranthes
4 Perpetual Roses.	3 Scented Geraniums.	6 Gladiolus.	4 Lobelias.
24 Verbenas.	2 Lemon Verbenas.	4 Double Geraniums.	2 Ageratum.
4 Heliotropes.	4 Scarlet Salvias.	6 Petunias.	2 Chrysanthemums.
4 Fuchsias.	2 Double Feverfew.	3 Dahlias.	2 Phloxes.
6 Zonale Geraniums.			

SELECTION No. 3.—$10. *Numbering 80 Plants.*

10 Monthly and Perpetual Roses.	4 Variegated Geraniums.	4 Petunias.	2 Coleus & Achyranthes
19 Verbenas.	3 Scented Geraniums.	2 Chrysanthemums.	4 Lantanas
3 Heliotrope.	2 Lemon Verbenas.	4 Double Tuberoses.	6 Gladiolus.
4 Fuchsias.	2 Scarlet Salvias.	2 Dahlias.	1 Caladium Esculentum.
6 Zonale Geraniums.	2 Double Feverfew.	2 Lobelias.	2 Ageratums.

SELECTION No. 4.—$5. *Numbering 40 Plants.*

4 Monthly Roses.	2 Zonale Geraniums.	1 Lemon Verbena.	2 Dahlias.
12 Verbenas.	2 Double Geraniums.	1 Scarlet Salvia.	2 Lobelias.
3 Heliotropes.	2 Variegated Geraniums	1 Blue Salvia.	2 Ageratums.
2 Fuchsias.	1 Rose Geranium.	2 Double Feverfew.	2 Coleus & Achyranthes.

VEGETABLE PLANTS.

	Per 100		Per 100
Asparagus Colossal, (Van Siclens)		Celery, (ready in July.)	
1 year old roots	$1 00	— Henderson's Dwarf White...	$ 75
— — (Van Siclens,) 2 year old		— Sandringham	1 00
roots	1 50	— Large White Solid	75
— Giant, 2 year old roots	1 00	— Hood's Red	1 00
Cabbage, Early (cold frame.)		— Turnip Rooted, (celeriac)	1 00
— — Jersey Wakefield	1 50	Horse Radish Sets	75
— — Winningstadt	1 50	Lettuce, (cold frame.)	
— — Oxheart	1 50	— Simpson, curled	1 00
— — York	1 50	— Boston Market, true	1 00
— — Flat Dutch	1 50	— (hot-bed,) the same kinds	50
— — Summer, (New,) for description, see Seed Catalogue	3 00	Egg Plant. Each. per doz. per 100	
— (hot-bed,) the same kinds, one-half the above rates.		— N. Y. Improved...10c. 1 00	6 00
— (Late,) ready in July.		— Black Pekin....'...10c. 1 00	6 00
— — Large Late Drumhead	75	Pepper.	
— Premium Flat Dutch	75	— Large Bell or Bull	
— Red (for pickling)	1 00	Nose...10c. 1 00	6 00
Cauliflower (cold frame.)		Rhubarb. Per doz.	
— Early Dwarf Erfurt	3 00	— Myatts Victoria	3 00
— — Paris	3 00	— Linnæus	3 00
— (hot-bed,) the same kinds.	1 50	Sweet Potatoes. Per 100	
— (Late,) ready in July.		— — Nansemond	75
— Paris	1 50	— — Southern Queen	1 00
— Erfurt	1 50	Tomatoes.	
		— Trophy, (from Headquarters Seed.) Per doz. 50c	3 00
		— Early Smooth Red. Per doz. 50c	3 00

Larger quantities, at special rates on application.

● STRAWBERRY PLANTS.

Triomphe de Gand. Per hundred.. $1 50 | Wilson's Albany. Per hundred.... $1 50

FOREIGN GRAPE VINES---FOR VINERIES.

These have been grown in pots, and are strong, healthy plants, and will be found to be of a quality entirely satisfactory. They can be safely sent any time before May 10th. Plants marked * are suitable for cold vineries.

Muscat, Canon Hall.—Bunches large, berries medium, amber white.
Muscat, Bowood.—Bunches large roundish oval, style of Muscat of Alexandria.
Muscat of Alexandria.—Large grape, of light golden color, the most popular of the white kinds.
Muscat, Blanc Hative.—Bunches medium, large golden white.
Black Hamburg.*--Sweet and juicy, a well-known excellent sort.
White Frontignac.*—Berries nearly white, bunch medium.
White Nice.—Bunch large, berries round, greenish white.
Santa Cruz.—Bunch and berry large, greenish white.
Calabrian Raison.—Bunches large and well formed, amber white.
Chasselas de Fontainbleau.—Medium bunch and berry, greenish white.
Prince Albert.—Black, berry and bunch large.
Lady Downes' Seedling.*—Bunch large, black berries, keeps a long while.
Charlesworth Tokay.—White, delicious flavor.
First size, extra strong, $2 each. Second size, fine plants, $1 each.

HARDY GRAPE VINES.---Ready 15th of May.

(Grown in three inch pots.)

Croton.—Bunch large, berry of medium size, light yellowish green, translucent, and in appearance and quality equal to the foreign grape; one of the earliest; 75c.

Concord.—"The Grape for the Million!" Black, large berry, sweet and aromatic. It succeeds on all soils, ripens in every season, is healthy and hardy, and gives bountiful crops under almost any kind of treatment. When only one variety is wanted, we invariably advise to plant Concord.

Delaware.—Red, bunches compact, berries small, sweet, and of most exquisite aroma. For quality there is no American grape to equal it.

Diana.—Red, bunches very compact, berries of average size; ripens with the Delaware; sweet and aromatic.

Early Black.—Resembles the Concord in style of growth and berry, ripening two weeks earlier.

Rogers, No. 9.—An excellent variety, berries medium, bunches rather small, color light bronze; a good bearer.

Rogers, No. 15.—Berries large, of a bronze color, bunches of good size and form; the best light grape of any.

Rogers, No. 17.—Resembles the preceding in size and general characteristics, but darker in color

Rogers, No. 22.—A splendid white grape, tinged with pink, of medium size, delicate flavor, the bunches well formed and compact; vine perfectly hardy, and free from mildew; 50c.

Rogers, Bronze.—A berry above the medium, bunches large, well formed, berry very sweet; 50c.

Rogers, No. 41.—An improvement on the Concord, berry of the same size, bunch larger and better formed, berries sweeter.

Rogers. No. 44—A splendid sort, berries large, black, bunch well shaped and compact, a good bearer, berry remaining on the vine a long time; a splendid sort.

Price of the above in three inch pots ready in May, 30 cents each, except where noted. Set of twelve for $3.

THE

AMERICAN AGRICULTURIST

Is a beautifully illustrated Journal, established in 1842, for the **Farm, Garden and Household,** including a special interesting and instructive Department for **Children and Youth.**

It is a large periodical of 44 pages, well printed, and filled with *plain, practical, reliable original* matter, including hundreds of *beautiful* **Engravings** in every annual volume.

It contains each month a calendar of Operations to be performed on the **Farm,** in the **Orchard, Garden,** and **Dwelling,** etc.

It comprises thousands of hints and suggestions, in every volume, prepared by practical, intelligent **working men,** who know what they write about.

It has a **Household Department,** valuable to every housekeeper, affording very many useful hints and directions calculated to lighten and facilitate in-door work.

It has a **Department for Children and Youth,** prepared with special care, to furnish not only amusement but also to inculcate knowledge and sound moral principles.

When the large expense involved in providing its interesting and varied reading matter, and its great number of superb Illustrations is considered, it is the

CHEAPEST PAPER IN THE WORLD.

Its subscription price is only **$1.50 a year;** *four* copies for $5; ten copies for $12; *twenty. or more,* $1 each; to which ten cents must be added and sent with *each subscription,* whether singly or in clubs, to pre-pay postage for the year 1873, which must be done in New York City, by the Publishers.

A large number of valuable and useful **Premiums** are offered to canvassers for the *American Agriculturist.* Send to the Publishers for an Illustrated Supplement, containing the Table of Terms, and full Descriptions of Premiums. Get your friends to join you, and **SUBSCRIBE TO-DAY.**

ORANGE JUDD COMPANY, Publishers,

245 Broadway, New York.

NEW YORK, January 1st, 1873.

I beg to state to my patrons, that I have agreed with the proprietors of the AMERICAN AGRICULTURIST to write exclusively for that paper, for the year 1873, such articles as I have been in the habit of writing for them for the past five years. These articles are mainly in response to questions that arise in matters pertaining to Horticulture, or to descriptions of *new Plants,* or *new Vegetables,* or to improvements in or new methods of their cultivation, as they arise in the prosecution of our large and varied business.

Peter Henderson

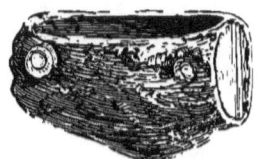

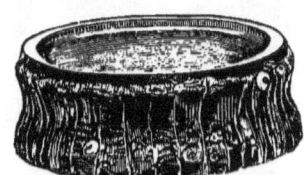

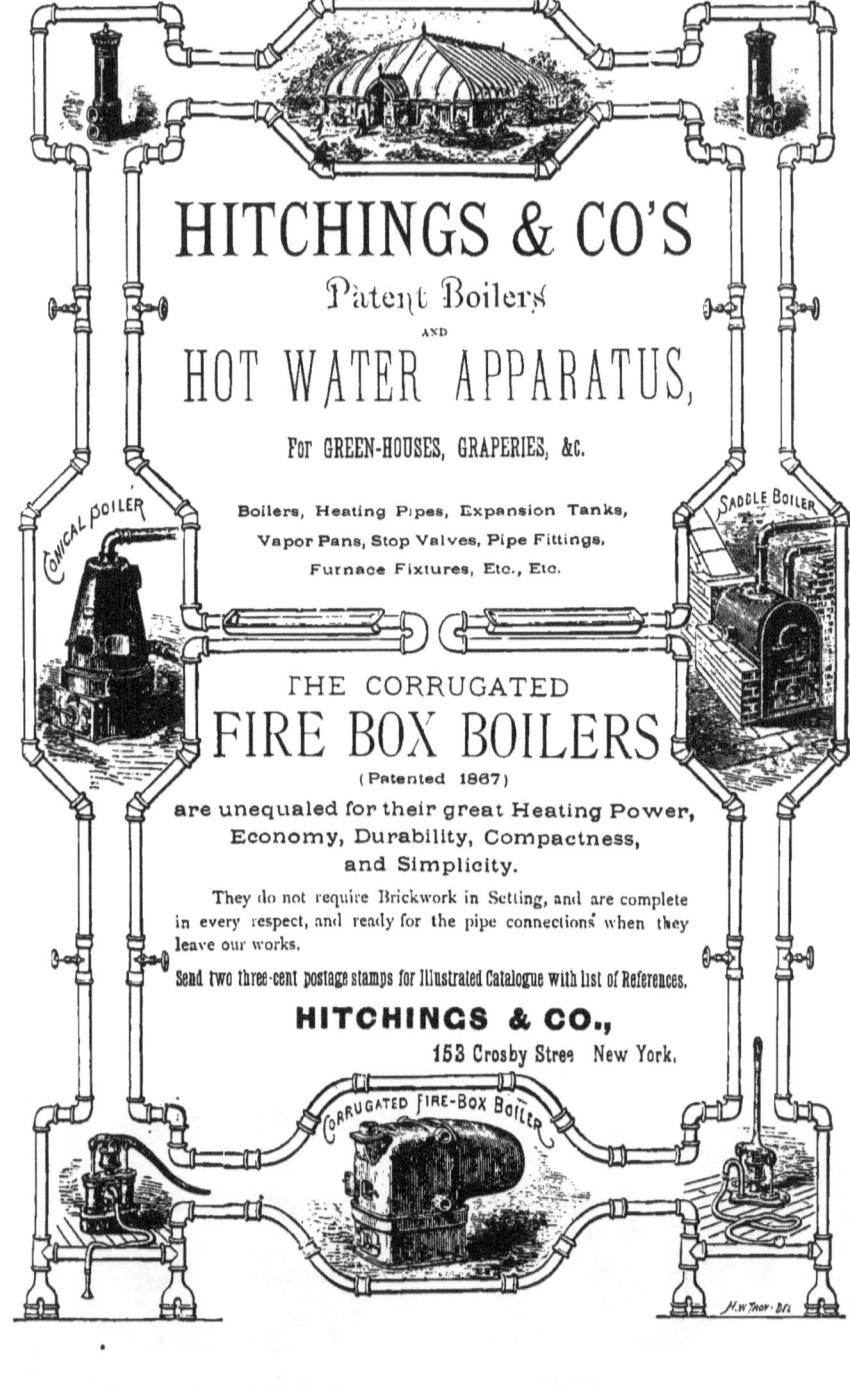

NEWLY REVISED AND ENLARGED EDITION
OF
Gardening for Profit
A WORK DEVOTED TO VEGETABLE GARDENING,
BY
Peter Henderson

Its teachings are our personal experience of over 20 years of growing vegetables for the great market of New York; and though mainly written for the market gardener, hundreds of amateurs and private gardeners have thanked us for its publication. Since the first edition, printed in 1866, upward of FIFTY THOUSAND COPIES have been sold. The subjects treated of are

Men fitted for the Business of Gardening.	Formation and Management of Hot-beds.
The Amount of Capital Required, and	Forcing Pits or Greenhouses.
Working Force per Acre.	Seeds and Seed Raising.
Profits of Market Gardening.	How, When and Where to Sow Seeds.
Location, Situation and Laying Out.	Transplanting, Insects.
Soils, Drainage and Preparation.	Packing of Vegetables for Shipping.
Manures, Implements.	Preservation of Vegetables in Winter.
Uses and Management of Cold Frames.	Vegetables, their Varieties and Cultivation.

SENT POST-PAID, PRICE, $1.50.

BY THE SAME AUTHOR:

Practical Floriculture.
NEW AND REVISED EDITION.

A Guide to the Successful Propagation and Cultivation of Florist's Plants.

In this work, which has everywhere become so deservedly popular, not only is the whole "art and mystery" of propagation explained, but the reader is taught how to plant and grow the plants after they have been propagated. The work is not one for florists and gardeners only, but the amateur's wants are constantly kept in mind, and we have a very complete treatise on the cultivation of flowers under glass, or in the open air, suited to those who grow flowers for pleasure as well as those who make them a matter of trade. The work is characterized by the same radical common sense that marked the author's "Gardening for Profit," and it holds a high place in the estimation of lovers of floriculture. The new edition has been thoroughly revised by the author, and much enlarged by the addition of valuable matter.

The following are a few of the subjects embraced in the latest edition : Laying out Flower Garden and Lawn ; Designs for Grounds and for Greenhouses ; Soils for Potting ; Cold Frames ; Hot-beds ; Greenhouses Attached to Dwellings ; Mode of Heating ; Propagation of Plants by Seeds and by Cuttings ; Culture of the Rose and Tuberose ; Growing of Winter-flowering Plants ; Construction of Bouquets, Baskets, etc.; Parlor and Window Gardening ; Wardian-cases and Ferneries ; Insects ; What Flowers Grow in the Shade ; Culture of Grape Vines under glass ; the Profits of Floriculture ; How to Become a Florist, etc., etc. BEAUTIFULLY ILLUSTRATED.

PRICE BY MAIL, POST-PAID, $1.50.

All purchasers of the above Books have their names entered on our list, and will receive our Catalogues of Seeds and Plants annually, free of charge.

PETER HENDERSON & CO., 35 Cortlandt St., New York.

INDEX.

FOR NEW PLANTS, SEE PAGES 1—20.